Patricia Wendorf was born in Somerset but, just before the Second World War, her parents moved to Loughborough, which is where she still lives. She is the author of the bestselling novels, LARKSLEVE and BLANCHE, which are the first two volumes of the *Patteran Trilogy* and which are largely based on her own family history.

Mrs Wendorf is a widow, and has tw four grandchildren.

# PATRICIA WENDORF

# Leo Days

Futura

For dear friends
Sheila, Isa, Andrea, and Sheila

A Futura Book

Copyright © 1984 by Patricia Wendorf

First published in Great Britain in 1984
by Hamish Hamilton Ltd, London

This edition published in 1987 by
Futura Publications, a Division of
Macdonald & Co (Publishers) Ltd
London & Sydney

ISBN 0 7088 3448 5

Printed in Great Britain by
The Guernsey Press Co. Ltd, Guernsey, Channel Islands

Futura Publications
A Division of
Macdonald & Co (Publishers) Ltd
Greater London House
Hampstead Road
London NW1 7QX

A BPCC plc Company

*Part One*

# WINTER

# 1.

The offices of Mainstay were housed in a converted Victorian villa, that stood in a narrow street, within sight and sound of St Joseph's steeple. On a quiet day she could hear the clock on the tower strike the quarter-hours, and the bells when they pealed for a wedding or tolled for a funeral.

The interview room was on the first floor, overlooking the street. The carpets and curtains were tobacco-brown, and the armchairs had yellow covers and wooden arms. The desk was a solid piece of office furniture, veneered in a stripey reddish wood. It held a phone, a wire tray for letters, a pottery jar filled with pencils, and a bud vase in which she tried to maintain a single fresh flower.

The conversion of the house had included gas central heating and a lot of white paintwork. The people who worked there supplied their own pictures and house-plants. Ruth had hung a framed print of Van Gogh's *Sunflowers* on the wall, because it looked cheerful; and encouraged a swiss-cheese plant to grow in a tub near the window.

When people asked what she did with her time, Ruth Flemming would say, 'Well – I suppose it's a kind of social work – really,' and then add quickly, 'but we're not

1

professional social workers. What we do is strictly voluntary. We try to help battered wives – elderly people at risk – bewildered parents – unsettled teenagers.'

The evasive note in her voice when she spoke about Mainstay, caused her mother's bridge-playing cronies to glance questioningly at her. As if they suspected her of trying to conceal some secret and faintly disreputable obsession.

The sky was that curious shade of dirty yellow that could only mean snow. It had hung suspended above the city since early morning, threatening to fall on somebody's head. People who were obliged to remain out of doors in the freezing temperatures were creeping along the pavements, heads ducked into their turned-up collars. Ruth turned back from the window, as the telephone rang.

A familiar voice said, 'Ah, is that Mainstay? Social Services here. Mrs Temple speaking. We were wondering if you could help us?' Competently and succinctly, the local authority lady explained her dilemma. 'A one-parent family, they've just moved into your area. We took action last month, and in spite of the grandmother's violent protestations, the three younger children are now in care. We've refrained from moving the eldest girl in the hope that she might rouse some latent spark of responsibility in her mother.' The cool voice warmed up with agitation. 'This mother has several charges against her. Drunkenness, theft, prostitution. On Christmas Eve she smashed up the Bridewell, and did actual damage to Sergeant McInnes.' She paused, 'Her family profess to be Romany gypsies. They were trapped just outside the city last month by that very wet weather. Her name is Delilah Smith. The child's name is Paisley.'

Although her appointment had been fixed for the next Monday morning, the gypsy sidled into Mainstay half an hour later looking as if she expected a gin-trap to close on her ankle. Delilah Smith was a thin, pale girl, with a headful of long, fair hair. She wore a shiny black raincoat, tightly belted, and purple suede fashion boots. Ruth invited her to sit down.

'Hello, Mrs Smith. You look very cold. Would you like some coffee?'

The girl gave one sly and contemptuous look, and then

lowered her eyelids.

'You can stuff yer coffee,' she said, 'drop o' gin 'ud keep the cold out!'

Ruth leaned back in her chair and considered Delilah, assigning to her the roles of drunkard, bawd, and wrecker of police stations. She quite literally did not appear to possess the physical stamina for such antics. 'Mrs Temple thought that it might be helpful if we had a talk about your problems.'

'Oh yeh? Well, stuff Mrs Temple!'

'Where are you living Mrs Smith?'

'Jus' round the corner. Number Twelve Nelson Street.'

'You have a house?'

'Yeh – a bloody house.' She mimicked perfectly the tones of the Local Authority social worker. 'If you want to keep Paisley with you, you must live where we put you.' Delilah subsided further into the armchair, was no more than a thin black line on the bright yellow cover.

'Paisley?' said Ruth, 'that's very unusual – and pretty.'

'Mistake, that were missus. We was travellin' in the North – Joe's a rigger wi' the fairground. Kid was born a bit unexpected like, an' we 'ant got no name picked out for her. I looked out the van, an' there was this signpost. "What's it say?" I asked Joe.'

'"Paisley," he said, "Paisley, Two miles."'

'What have the Social Services supplied you with, so far, Mrs Smith?'

'Bits an' pieces.' The girl shrugged. 'We was cold over Christmas so we chopped 'em all up for the fire.'

'So we start off from scratch?'

'If you like. I don' care all that much.'

'Monday morning,' said Ruth, 'I'll come round and see you. Make a list of essentials.'

Delilah stood up. 'I 'ant got no money. Any chance of a sub?' Her eyes were on Ruth's leather handbag. 'You got a interestin' face, missus. I could tell you –'

'No,' Ruth said sharply; and then quietly, 'No, Mrs Smith. I don't believe in fortune-telling, thank you.'

'You don' believe in me, eh? Then I'll tell you fer nothin'. You got some trouble comin', lady.'

The day closed down abruptly in mid-afternoon, and Sam

3

Bright who was Mainstay's Assistant Organiser, advised Ruth to leave the city at once before the weather worsened.

She manoeuvered her car through the narrow streets of St Joseph's: past the cinemas and their peeling posters; past the hostels for the temporarily homeless, and the cheap lodging houses which housed a large proportion of Mainstay's regular clients.

A child called Paisley was living in one of these drab and draughty streets; snatched from her grandmother, and the caravan which must, until lately, have been her home.

A short cut through the closed-down fruit and vegetable market, brought her into that quarter of the city which was inhabited almost solely by Asians. Down here, the shop windows were packed with garish colour. She could see rainbow saree-lengths draped over models; sets of glittering rhinestone jewellery displayed on black velvet; brass clocks and trays; gold pendants and bracelets; carved elephants; and the smiling faces of strange gods.

Because of the freezing weather, the curry-houses had opened up earlier than usual, and behind the rows of rubber plants in their steamed-up windows, the Bengalis were already doing brisk business. A few young women pushed prams on the bitter streets; their golden faces tinged blue with the cold. Below the hems of their thick winter coats, the iridescent sarees gleamed and shimmered in the fading light. They reminded her of emergent butterflies, caught halfway out of brown tweed chrysalises by the sudden frost, and doomed to live out their lives forever in the wrong place, and in the wrong season.

She flicked a switch on the dashboard and a voice chattered softly, some young and cheerful disc-jockey, snug in his overheated cubicle, was predicting an imminent blizzard with temperatures down below zero. On reaching the city outskirts she increased her speed.

Up in the Hillcrest district the streets were wide, with broad clean pavements and grass verges. As she turned the car towards Spinney Hill the first indecisive snowflakes began to drift gently across her windscreen. The snow seemed reluctant to fall, and then, all at once, a gusting wind sprang up, bringing with it the unmistakable whirling white of a definite blizzard.

Ruth switched off the radio, and turned on the windscreen wipers. She was a nervous driver even in clear sunny weather. Within seconds, her visibility had been rendered non-existent, and the wipers were whining and faltering under the weight of the snow.

She tried to think about Greece, last summer. Was it any wonder that the people who lived in the southern latitudes seemed able to take a more philosophical view of life? In late August, or early September, she sometimes flew south with her sister Georgina, to the sunshine of Italy, or the Greek islands; and these were the Leo Days. The lazy days of hot, bright sunlight.

She drove slowly, trying hard to keep the guiding kerb-stone in view. At the same time a quite separate part of her mind was still roaming the dusty streets of Heraklion on a summer's morning. It was not until she got out of the car to unlatch them, that she noticed the gates of her driveway; wide open and swinging loose in the storm. The sight made her feel uneasy. She was sure that Harry, no matter how pre-occupied he had been before leaving, would never have neglected to close those gates.

She garaged the Mini, and ran the short distance across to the stormporch. The snow was settling thickly now on the lawn and driveway. She stamped her caked shoes on the doormat, and began to unlock the front door.

As she turned the key, Ruth was seized with a sure premonition that something was wrong in the house. It was such a strong feeling that she ran from the stormporch and peered down over Spinney Hill with some wild idea of fetching a neighbour. But the snow was coming down heavily now; and all she could see was a patchy outline of uneven rooftops.

She thought she could hear Delilah's voice, driven on the wind, 'You don' believe in me, eh? Then I'll tell you fer nothing'. You got some trouble comin' lady.'

She went back to the stormporch, took firm hold of the doorkey, and turned it. Heavy snow, she recalled, had frequently made her neurotic. Under blizzard conditions she was quite capable of conjuring up bloodstains on the kitchen walls, and bodies littering up her hallway.

In fact, what she actually saw as the door swung open, was

5

a deeply-indented patch of blue carpet, where her husband's golf-clubs had stood for the past ten years. There was another empty space on the wall where his Lowry painting had hung that morning. She began to smile. Was it possible that in spite of the system of locks and alarms he had lately installed, Harry's house had been burgled?

She walked through the hall and into the drawing-room, switching on lamps and overhead lights as she went. She braced herself to discover the silver cabinet empty, and her tiny collection of porcelain missing – but no! It was all as secure as when she had left it, that morning. Her Nymphenburg rooster still arched his tiny tail-feathers, and the lady from Meissen still sat on her separate shelf. It was only the bookcases that had been plundered in this room. The dark shelving loomed over her, gap-toothed in the lamp-light. Ruth reached for her reading glasses, and studied the remaining titles. She was not really surprised to discover that all of the missing volumes belonged to Harry, her husband.

She went back to the hall and studied the dent in the carpet. It was a darker shade of blue than the rest of the broadloom, and she felt a pang of regret at the way the expensive Wilton had faded. Nothing lasted forever. No matter how high had been the initial outlay.

It had always been a quiet house. It possessed that quality of expensive silence that is achieved by efficient double-glazing, the insulation of thick carpets, and an absence of pets, and children.

Within the walls, the sound of the storm was muted, and she could hear the fridge hum softly, and then switch itself off. The radiators were giving off those little crackling noises that they usually made in cold weather, and she leaned on the newel-post for a moment, thankful for the normality of familiar sounds.

At the top of the stairs she decided to dispense with surprise altogether. She was resigned to finding more empty spaces on the bathroom shelves. Up here, several bottles were missing. Hair-tonic, aftershave, mouthwash. She opened the doors of the medicine cabinet, and saw that his vast stock of patent remedies had been removed. Harry had even taken his old holiday sponge-bag, and the nearly-bald toothbrush he flatly refused to discard.

She paused at the next door. A faint smell of paint and new wallpaper still came from the bedroom. On an impulse last month, she had selected shades of romantic pink. A Sanderson print of rosebuds and rampant ivy. A new bedhead in a trendy wicker design of hearts-entwined. An off-white carpet, and blush-tinted mirrors. It had been the kind of last-ditch attempt at reviving a dying marriage that is recommended by the women's magazines on their back pages. Well – so much for decor!

The letter, thrown carelessly onto the duvet, lay on her side of the bed. For once in his life, conventional Harry had not run quite true to form by pinning it to her pillow. Four words had been scrawled on the plain white paper. 'I am sorry Ruth.'

The apology, and its location, was she thought, pretty apt, considering the state of her marriage. Well, she would hardly need to look any further. His wardrobes and drawers had been emptied, right down to the very last cufflink. She moved over to the window, and looked down at the darkening garden. The snow was still falling, humping the weeping-willow tree more distinctly into its permanent stance of misery.

So this is how it felt to be a deserted wife. The women who consulted Mainstay had partners who departed from home as regularly as trains: towards other women, other cities, into prison. It was not really a problem she had ever expected to face in her own life.

Beneath the street lights she could see how the bushes and branches of trees were bowed low by the weight of the snow. A worried looking dog ran across her driveway, confused by the whiteness. In that hour between daylight and darkness, many things had changed.

# 2.

He had been over-solicitous towards her that morning. He had warned her of icy roads, had urged her to leave the house a little earlier than usual; had promised to wash-up the breakfast dishes for her.

Her moment of true shock came when she entered the kitchen. The table was exactly as she had left it; a clutter of empty egg-shells, sticky marmalade spoons, and scattered toast crumbs. Her careful indifference shattered into splinters of rage. She beat her clenched fists on the kitchen table, until the blue cups rattled in their saucers, and the cutlery chattered.

She began to clear the table. She scraped violently at congealed egg on plates and silver; tossed china perilously into scalding water; screwed the tablecloth into a ball of knotted orange, and aimed it at a row of copper saucepans. He had subjected her to the ultimate insult. Denied her the satisfaction of confrontation. Harry had absented himself without a by-your-leave. He had sneaked away in an unguarded moment, without giving her fair notice of intent.

She pressed her palms against the cold surface of the stainless-steel drainer, and then lifted them up to cool her burning face. She forced herself to breathe in and out, very slowly and deeply. Ashamed, and faintly embarrassed by the undignified childishness of her outburst, Ruth began the familiar preparations for the scratch-meal she usually ate in Harry's absence.

She plugged in the kettle, switched on the toaster, fetched eggs and butter from the pantry, and began to cut bread. The knife was quite steady in her hand, and the wholemeal slices tipped over, straight and even from the loaf.

She sat down with her meal at the kitchen table, and at once fell into the trap of conjecture that is waiting for every woman who finds herself in a similar position. She began the wild search for pointers. His unexplained absences from the factory. A slight change in his manner towards her. The more youthful style in the way he dressed; and combed his hair.

The faint hint she had sometimes caught, of Arpège on his clothing.

She had known about Harry's women. Of course she had. Marriage for her, had involved a certainty of heartbreak, and any woman who denied such knowledge was either a fool, or a liar. She tried to work out what it was she had lost, and then wondered if she had any right to an opinion. To have suffered loss must surely have implied possession, in the first place. The egg congealed upon the toast, and she pushed her plate away.

He appeared to have removed every item from the house that he might reasonably lay claim to; two cars, at least, would have been required to load up all that booty. This assumed premeditation; careful planning, and almost certainly, an accomplice. She could imagine how it must have been. Having watched her pull out of the driveway that morning; having waved her goodbye in his usual manner, her husband would have picked up the phone and summoned his friend. Then Harry, a fine presence in his Austin Reed sweater and pressed Daks trousers, would have master-minded the entire operation. She could just see him stripping shelves and cupboards, handing selected objects to his companion, who would have been required to pack, and carry the loaded suitcases out to the cars. She hoped that this girl was accustomed to burdens. Harry was not – nor had he ever been – a willing hefter of heavy baggage.

She tipped the unwanted meal into the waste-bin, and began, absent-mindedly, to wash up the single plate, the cup and saucer. This, she supposed, was to be her blue-print for the future. There would be no more shirts to iron, no extra shopping. No special meals to plan, for this or any other weekend. The fact that she would no longer need to search the supermarket shelves for his favourite brand of pickle, could take on the dimensions of a disaster, if she allowed it to do so.

Confrontation of some sort was a daily experience for the women who sought the help of Mainstay. She had simply wanted her life to be neat and tidy. Tag-ends of unresolved emotion disturbed her. She had even thought it was possible to domesticate uncomfortable suspicion; to collect bits of antique silver in the place of niggling resentment. Her sister

9

Georgina always wore Arpège. But then, so did several thousand other women.

Automatically, she set the burglar alarms and slid home the bolts and locks on the doors and windows. The snow had muffled all sound in the streets and gardens – but the house still listened. She switched on the radio and at once the rooms were full of the throb of guitars, and a girl's voice singing. 'The summer days are dying, The birds are on the wing...'

Ruth felt a pang, and pressed her hand to the spot where she thought her heart might be. She at once felt foolish and melodramatic; after all, she had never really loved Harry; the pang she had felt must have been for hot, summer days.

The house felt empty, and she wondered, lightheadedly, if her husband's belongings had, alone, confirmed his existence in her life. Take away the books, the golf-clubs, the patent remedies, and the rows of expensive clothing – and where was he? It had been a polite kind of marriage, right down to the final four words with which he had written himself out of her story. If she had a friend, thought Ruth, this would be the right time to phone her. They could have sipped their Martini's while they stripped Harry bare. They could have hung him up on a hook of invective; condemned, and passed judgement upon him in his absence.

But she had no friends. She had acquaintances, colleagues, a sister; women who would mention Tolerance and Under-standing, and the advisability of allowing a forty-year-old husband his Final Fling. She passed time by re-arranging the bedroom, transferring the clothes from her own cluttered wardrobes to that side of the room that had always been Harry's territory. She grabbed up his pillows and hurled them against the far wall; then positioned her own two pillows, dead centre beneath the entwined-wicker-hearts.

She switched off the lamp, pulled back the curtain, and looked into the garden. The snow was still falling.

# 3.

The early morning radio programmes were full of the drama of the bitter weather. Main roads were blocked, telephone wires were down, villages cut off, power cuts threatened, and more snow was forecast. But Harry would have shown forethought. He would, at this moment, be tucked up cosily with his companion in some motorway motel room, or prearranged honeymoon cottage. He was careful about his health; fussy over food and clean beds, and preserving his physical well-being. He would never accompany her to Greece or Italy. He had doubted the cleanliness of the sheets, and said that unusual food would upset his stomach; and in any case, Ruth should know that excessive heat always brought him out in unpleasant rashes.

She showered, dressed, and pinned up her long black hair; even though it was Saturday, and no one would see her. The house shrank away from her this morning as if it could hope to conceal the gaps and omissions left by Harry. The carriage clock was missing – he had also taken the poacher and the egg-timing gadget. She remembered his childish faith in the lightly-boiled egg, and was not at all surprised. The bills, she noticed, were still clipped in position on the top shelf of his bureau.

While the coffee perked and the bacon grilled, she fell into her old habit of trying to rationalise her husband. With a bit of juggling and a deft adjustment, it should be just possible for her to categorise him as a failed investment. Strange, how in the end it always came back to money. Up here in The Mullions, or down in Sebastopol Street, in the Mainstay building, what counted was, who had it, or needed it, or would cheat and lie to obtain it.

Harry Flemming had always wanted money.

She remembered the day he first came to The Mullions, and the hesitant smile and deferential twist of his body, as her father introduced him.

'Our new accountant,' her father had said, 'just up from London, and finding life in the Midlands a bit quiet.' She had

11

seen the way Harry looked around him; at the paintings and silver, at the carpets, and the oversized radiators; at her mother's extravagant arrangements of out-of-season flowers. She had seen the question turn over slowly behind his eyes as they settled on her left hand, third finger.

They had used the small sitting-room that weekend. Her mother seated on the blue brocade sofa, because it matched her eyes, had poured Earl Grey tea from a silver pot into rosebud china. She had smiled coquettishly at Harry with her coral-pink lips, and arched her thin eyebrows at him. Seated at his ease in a tall wing chair, a white napkin draped across one knee, Harry had eaten the egg and cress sandwiches and Victoria sponge cake very slowly, as if he needed to prolong the visit. Her mother had dropped cubed sugar into teacups with chased-silver tongs, and proffered thin slices of lemon on a filigreed dish. She had flirted as outrageously with the new accountant as she did with most men.

Harry's attitude had been subdued and respectful. But when he set his plate down and dabbed at his lips, Ruth suspected that he was laughing behind the lace-edged napkin. Her first act, on inheriting The Mullions from her father, had been to pack away the silver tea service, and rosebud china, and buy mugs and a big brown teapot from Woolworths'. Harry had been angry with her. 'One of my nicest memories', he had said, 'is of your mother, poised at the antique tea-trolley, the Georgian teapot in her hand.'

He had been deeply impressed with the house on that first visit. In the drawing-room he had halted before Georgina's portrait. 'Your sister?'

'Yes. That's Georgina.'

'She has a look of you about her.'

'Don't be ridiculous,' she had snapped, 'there's no likeness.'

As they moved through her father's house, she had become achingly aware of the new accountant. When they reached the staircase, she had deliberately motioned him to ascend before her. She had wanted to study the set of his shoulders, the glossy brown hair that curled onto his collar, and the pull of grey worsted across his buttocks.

'Yes,' she had told him, 'it is a large bathroom. Yes, the tiles are hand painted. That design of mermaids and dolphins is rather unusual.' Later on, they had stood in the porch, a united family. As they wished their agreeable guest good-night, Ruth had measured his height, unobtrusively, against her own. He was quite a tall man. He topped her by at least two inches. Even then, at that first meeting, it had seemed painfully important.

Saturday passed slowly; muffled in snow and old memories. The house grew larger by the hour. The rooms and the corridors stretched out and multiplied like mirror images, all around her. Life would go on, with Harry – or without him. He had left no reminder of himself, no memento. Not a cufflink, nor a handkerchief. Not a child. But she had not reckoned with emptiness; with the mere displacement of air that his presence had caused when he lived there.

She dragged the wing-chair from the sitting-room, and hid in the kitchen beside the all-night boiler. She fell asleep, unable to face the long haul up the staircase to the honey-moon-pink of the room she had once shared with Harry.

Normality returned with Monday morning. Concentration was needed to negotiate the steep and icy driveway, and she was thankful to be fighting the steering-wheel, bumping and grinding among the frozen ruts made by earlier travellers. The snow lay deep and white on the hedges and lawns of the Hillcrest district. Children in bright woollen caps and mufflers threw snowballs at one another on their way to school. The houses of the wealthy were discreetly dug-in behind tall stands of established oak and pine. Long drive-ways and wrought-iron gates were intended to discourage the riff-raff: only the most dedicated of scroungers had ever completed the marathon course to her father's front door.

The roads had been cleared in the city centre, and she found herself driving against the usual tide of week-end rubbish that littered the streets of St Joseph's. But, this morning, the beer-cans rolling in gutters, and the chip papers flapping around lampposts seemed to steady her mind. In Sebastopol Street, the snow was reduced to a hazard of black, frozen lumps on the pavements. No children played there.

Several bundles of discarded clothing had been brought over from St Joseph's church hall: the unsold remnants of last

13

Saturday's jumble sale. From nine until eleven, she dispensed thick sweaters and topcoats. She searched anxiously for the near-fit; suggested the possible adjustment. Ruth pulled the despised and hideous garments from the big cardboard box, crying, 'Look! This will probably do for you. You can move the buttons, let out the seams, shorten the hemline. Well – the colour suits you!' She advised adaption of everything, from skimpy raincoats, to overlarge shoes, to worn-out emotions.

It was all relative. When you had nothing, your standards were necessarily lowered. You were obliged to compromise. You accepted the unsound, the defective, the second-rate, the sub-graded.

Georgina had once said, jokingly of course, that because of her height there were only a few professions to which Ruth was eminently suited. She had even listed them in appropriate order. Police-woman, Hospital Matron, Prison wardress.

## 4.

The houses in Nelson Street were reserved for the city's problem families. She drove through a street of well cared for terraced houses, turned a corner, and immediately entered a wasteland. The Council workmen had dug several holes in the road, and then gone away, mysteriously; never, it seemed, to return. Bits of St Joseph's were always being torn down, or dug up, or rearranged in some way. Someone had painted 'WOGS GO HOME', in large white letters on an end wall. It was very demoralizing. It was not wise to walk down here alone, after dark. Even now, in full daylight, she double-checked that her car was securely locked.

Her appointment with Delilah Smith had been set for eleven-thirty. Before setting out Ruth had packed the boot of the Mini with a paraffin heater, a can of oil, and a few threadbare Army blankets. Sam had shown her Delilah

Smith's documentation. In her twenty-six years the gypsy had been dealt with, referred back from, handed onto, and given up by, an incredible number of policemen and social workers in most of the northern counties of Britain. In her time as a volunteer worker with the Mainstay bureau, the 'travellers' were a species Ruth had not yet encountered.

The lock on the door of Number Twelve was broken. She knocked several times, but nobody answered, and so she pushed at the rotting brown woodwork, and walked straight in. She found Delilah Smith in a ground floor room at the rear of the house, seated on a beercrate while her child stoked the fire with the highly polished leg of a dining-room table. A stained mattress and a heap of old coats lay in a corner; the rest of the room was quite empty. The house reeked of damp and bad drains.

'Hello, Mrs Smith –' she began. Without saying a word Delilah vacated the beercrate and slouched across the room to sit crosslegged on the mattress. Ruth sat down on the broad wooden slats, her long legs tucked up uncomfortably, so that her chin almost rested on her knees.

'Mrs Smith –' she began again, 'that front door worries me. It's not safe for you and your little girl to be here alone in an unlocked house.'

Delilah jerked her head backwards, towards the street. 'They 'ont touch me, missus.'

'How can you be certain?'

Delilah grinned. 'They know better'n that.' She wriggled with self-satisfaction. 'They say I got the evil eye.'

'And have you?'

'Happen you'll fine out fer yersel', if you 'ant careful.'

Ruth tried to regain some hold on the strange conversation. 'Now look Mrs Smith –'

'Call me Della. Everybody else do.'

'Very well, then. Della. I saw your casenotes this morning, and it seems that the Social Services supplied you with perfectly adequate furniture when you moved in here; including two electric heaters. I should like to know what has happened to them.'

'Like I told you, lady. We was cold – so we burned 'em.'

'But you can't burn electric convectors. Where are they Della?'

The answer rose up, like a prayer, from the hearthstone. Paisley Smith spoke out, without bothering to turn her head. 'We 'ant got no money for the meter, so we flogged 'em. What good is 'lectric thingys when you 'ant got no money.' The gruff little voice had a note of authority in it. As if it were she, and not Della, who made all the important decisions.

'But Paisley,' Ruth argued, 'you receive a heating allowance with your Social Security payments.'

The child pointed at her mother with blunt, sooty fingers. 'She needs fags and gin, or else she gets stroppy.' Paisley looked protectively at Della. 'Gin is good for most things. Don' you know that?'

Ruth got up from the beercrate and moved closer to the fireplace. Someone had cared for Paisley Smith at some time in her life; she was tall and sturdy for a ten-year-old girl. Her small snub features were heavily freckled, and the fierce ginger hair was braided into a single rough plait. Paisley grabbed up a piece of the dining-room table and threatened Ruth with it. 'I can look out fer her better'n you can. Why'nt you just bugger-off?'

Della went into the kitchen. Ruth could hear her rattling the teacups and filling the kettle. She could only suppose that the Social Services crockery, being non-combustible, had escaped the holocaust. Paisley abandoned the table leg, but still looked mutinous.

'How do you "look-out" for your mother?'

'Shan't tell you.'

'Why not?'

'She can't help it can she?' the child burst out, 'if she 'ant very good at some things.'

'What sort of things?'

'Just you shut up, that's all. You're nosier than them bloody coppers!'

Della came back, carrying a battered metal teapot, and three cracked bone-china teacups, but no saucers. 'Drink up, now,' she ordered, suddenly cheerful. 'I'll tell you your luck. I'm good wi' the tea leaves.'

Ruth drank Della's tea with difficulty; averting her eyes from the mouse-droppings in the sugar, and the crust of soured milk on the rim of the bottle. She went out to the car, taking Paisley with her. They collected the paraffin heater, the can of oil, and the blankets. 'These are not to be pawned or sold,' she said firmly.

On the doorstep, Della Smith, quite predictably asked her for money. Ruth looked at the child. 'Have you eaten yet, Paisley?'

The child shook her head. Ruth took two pound notes from her handbag. 'Fetch fish and chips. Don't be long now. I shall stay here until you come back.'

In a ground floor room of the Mainstay building, there was always a small stock of furniture that had been donated; each item was in keen demand, and on her return to the office, Ruth checked up on available items.

She discovered a worn red carpet. A table and two shabby armchairs. Two divan-bases, but only one mattress; and a battered old wardrobe with an insecure door, and cracked mirror. It did not look like much on which to build a new life; but it would be an improvement on the collection of Tesco bags that presently contained the Smith family's clothing.

There was no word from Harry. But she did not, she told herself sharply, really believe that there would be. But still she ran to the phone every time it rang; and flipped her way anxiously through the morning letters. She tried to think of the hours since Harry's defection as being post-existent; a kind of resurrection. In terms of a good time that was coming. She tried not to think about the possible lies he had told her.

She hauled the brush along her length of thick black hair, and folded it deftly into a neat French pleat. She jabbed the metal pins into the familiar weight upon her neck without ever needing to glance into the mirror. Ruth's dressing-table held none of those scented pots and bottles which seemed so essential to her mother and Georgina. She was secretly proud of her lack of personal vanity, and the fact that she simply washed her face with soap and water.

She put on the plain white blouse, the navy-blue tailored suit, the low-heeled Oxfords. Her 'soup-kitchen outfit', Georgina called it. She had made plans to visit Billy Evans on that Tuesday morning, in the St Joseph's Working Men's

Hostel. Billy was a skilled joiner and locksmith, and one-time client of Mainstay. Out of gratitude for past favours, and a pressing need for employment, he was willing to do the odd jobs which the larger firms in the area refused to undertake. The Hostel was clean and warm, if a little spartan. Billy asked her to sit down, and offered a cigarette, which she declined. Aged about thirty-five, Billy Evans was known to the officers of the local Bridewell as a man who indulged in periodic and disastrous bouts of drinking.

'I have a little job for you, Billy. A house in Nelson Street that needs to be made secure. Good locks on the doors and windows – but you know the sort of thing I mean.'

He grinned and nodded. 'Well, I'll try miss. But them old houses are falling to pieces. They need iron bars on the windows down there.'

'How is life treating you these days, Billy?'

'Can't grumble miss. Gets a bit lonely, like. But I keeps breathing in and out.'

Ruth found herself studying the man more closely than usual. Listening for the pain behind the words. Billy favoured the trendy image. He wore a silver cross in one ear, tight jeans, and an amazing sweater with a slogan printed on it, which invited the reader to 'KEEP ON TRUCKIN'.

'No girl-friend Billy?'

He fingered the cross in his ear-lobe. 'It's the booze, see miss. I'm OK when I'm sober. But you know that, don't you?' He looked distressed. 'It's like this, see. Nice girls won't have me.'

'You'll find somebody,' Ruth consoled him. But she knew what he meant.

'Number Twelve, Billy,' she said briskly, 'and I'll be obliged if you'll go there today. The occupants are a young gypsy-woman and her child. She seems to believe that the "evil eye" will subdue her neighbours, but I shall feel happier when there are locks on her doors.'

Billy raised an eyebrow. 'Sounds like Della?'

'Yes, it is. Do you know her?'

He smiled, broadly. 'Who don't know her, miss? She's a very "friendly" sort – if you takes my meaning.'

Harry was a natty dresser. He had always understood what

suited him best, and then made quite certain of being able to afford it. He had taken with him the matching set of cowhide luggage, with the monogram stamped in gold on each piece. In it he had packed the pure-silk shirts and pyjamas. The wild-silk crimson robe with embroidered dragons; the camel's-hair overcoat, and the cashmere sweaters. There had been outfits for golf and tennis hanging in his wardrobes; evening dress; sporty hats and a topper. Shoes for every possible occasion.

A bright green quilted jacket in a shop window; and she was halting the Mini on double-yellow lines in order to peer at the price. She parked the car less riskily, just around the corner, and ran back to the shop to find a matching green woollen cap with white tassels, sheepskin mittens and two pairs of thick, warm trousers.

Ruth paid for her contraband goods, and concealed them beneath a plaid rug in the boot of the car. She planned to insert the new items in between an old school raincoat and a few shrunken jumble sale woollens. She would see Della's child when she opened the parcel; see her face light up.

Because of the snow, the schools had closed early, and Ruth timed her arrival in Nelson Street to coincide with that of Paisley Smith. Billy Evans had been there before her. There were strong new locks on the doors, and firm catches on all the old windows. A couple of sacks of chopped firewood stood in the hallway, and a wood fire crackled on the hearthstone. The red carpet had been delivered with the rest of the furniture, and Billy had repaired the wardrobe and stood it in the corner.

'This looks better,' Ruth said brightly, 'More home-like.'

Della shrugged. 'It 'ant like the 'van,' she muttered. Della's mood had changed since their last meeting. She was full of a tense elation that made her contemptuous of Ruth. She stared at the lady from Mainstay for some moments, and then said, keenly, 'Don' know much about my sort, do you "gorgio" woman?'

Ruth was careful to ignore the child who was down on the carpet unpacking the parcel. Paisley held up the new green coat, the hat and gloves, and the thick worsted trousers. Della's gaze moved from Ruth, to the jubilant child, and back again. She tipped her head sideways. 'Fond o' kids, 'ant you? Bought them new clothes out of your own pocket, I reckon. Bloody good o' you, that were,' she paused, and a tight little grin twitched one side of her mouth. 'Got no kids of your own, have you, lady?'

Ruth said, 'No. I don't have any children.' Curiosity about Della; the disconcerting switch she was capable of making from crass stupidity, to sudden, intuitive observation, led Ruth into saying, 'You're quite right of course. I don't know very much about your sort of people. Would you like to tell –?'

Della's eyes came wide open. 'It'll cost yer,' she interrupted. 'Lay a couple o'quid on the table, an' I'll tell about about it.' She banged down the teapot like an auctioneer's gavel. 'There now! That's a better offer than I give them old cows in the Social Office.'

Bribery led to corruption. The money would be spent on gin. Ruth reached for her handbag, and still caught in the spin of Delilah's light-green gaze, she laid two pound notes on the table.

Della Smith was a born story-teller. A spinner of yarns in the old word-of-mouth tradition. She made use of the pause and the gesture: the dramatic flourish. She was also, according to Mrs Temple, an inveterate liar.

'My Gran's the Queen of the Gypsies. I were born on the straw underneath her vardo.'

'Vardo?'

Della described an arc with one hand. 'You know – them old vans, pulled wi' horses. She's rich my Gran is. Got more'n you gorgios.'

'What about your mother?'

'Dunno. Never see her.'

'And your father?'

Della stared at the fire and seemed strangely unwilling to continue.

'Your father,' Ruth persisted, 'what was he like?'

'He were gorgio.'

'What does that mean exactly?'

Della grew impatient. 'Like you. Not Romani, not one of us. He died when I were a little 'un.'

'So you lost both your parents?'

Della's tone was indifferent. 'Makes no odds, do it? My ma

run off – but my Gran brung me up.' She lowered her lids and glanced sideways at Ruth. 'But you 'ant paid me good money to hear about all that old stuff, have yer? What you really wants to know, is all about Joe Smith an' me.'

Ruth could not deny it. 'Yes,' she said, 'I would like to hear about Joe.'

Della moved in the armchair, huddled closer to the fire. 'Joe goes roun' wi' the fair,' she said softly, 'he's a rigger' a gorgio.' She hooted, abruptly, at the memory. 'Bloody carrots, Joe were! Frizzy ginger hair, an' plastered all over wi' freckles.' She nodded her head in the child's direction. 'That one there looks jus' like him.' She paused, then said sadly, 'Never did know what I see in him, missus.'

'How old were you –?'

'Sixteen. He were twenty. Oh, we done it all legal. Register Office, white frock, wedding ring. He were good to me, sometimes.'

'Then why –?'

'Too many bloody kids – that's why.' Della's thin face twisted at the memory. 'But a lady like you don' go in for them mud-larks very often. You looks the frightened sort as 'ud keep her legs together.' She thumped the armchair, and giggled. 'But I knows a bit better these days. I got clever. He were handy wi' his fists too, Joe were. Put me in hospital more'n once, Joe did.' She regarded Ruth's tight features with something near to pity. 'Don' know much about men, do yer missus?'

Ruth said, 'So that's why you left him?'

Della looked surprised. 'Not me! Bastard cleared off one night, wi'out saying so much as a quick cheerioh.' She frowned. 'Fairground folk never liked me. Said I brought 'em bad luck. So I come back to Gran.'

'And then –?'

Della stood up abruptly. 'An' then nothin'. Don' you try an' push me lady. You can clear off now. You had your two quids' worth.'

It had been her father's decision that Ruth should marry Harry Flemming. Not overtly. The family code didn't operate on that honest level. The new accountant and she had been juxtapositioned, manoeuvered, drawn artfully together.

People had said she was lucky to get him; for, as her mother pointed out, good-looking bachelors of the right type were not likely to be found on the public wards of the city hospital.

Her mother had disapproved of nursing as Ruth's chosen career. She had complained of the pervasive odour of antiseptic, and advised spraying with Chanel No 5 as a means of disguising the smell. At the age of twenty-eight, unattached and conspicuously lonely, Ruth was aware that she rested quite heavily on her parents' hands.

Nothing fails like failure; and as her sister Georgina grew more fetching with every month that passed, Ruth became more than ever disinclined to compete. She wanted to get married and have children; but she was suspicious of emotional upheaval. Being kissed goodnight on the doorstep was quite pleasant; or even grappling for two or three purple minutes on the back seat of somebody's car. Georgina had said that Ruth was too timid; but as she had tried to explain, her reluctance to indulge in what she termed 'sex before marriage' could not even be put down to an excess of virtue. Ruth had vacillated; she trembled on the brink. Another, and more limiting, factor that governed her love life was her extraordinary height. She stood six feet and one inch in her stockinged feet and, like many tall girls, she exerted a certain macabre fascination over very small men. The ludicrous possibilities of the situaton appalled her; so that Harry Flemming, handsome, approved by her father, and a fortuitous six foot three inches, was, in the end, accepted by her as a bargain she could not reasonably refuse.

Harry had treated her with old-world respect. He was civil and urbane. Social tact was his hallmark. She could not imagine that Harry had ever been moved to wrestle a girl in the back of his car; he seemed so unruffled, so band-box fresh, so untouched by human hand. On their wedding night he made love to her so politely, that she was tempted to ask if that was all there was to it – but felt that she hardly knew him well enough on that first occasion to be quite so bluntly critical of him.

Georgina and Harry had loathed one another on sight. They both said so. Ruth had worried about it. 'I want them to be friends,' she had said to her mother, 'it makes things so awkward.' But Mrs Maynard had looked at her oddly and muttered something inappropriate about 'letting sleeping dogs lie.' Georgina had visited The Mullions only rarely after Ruth married Harry.

5.

There are secrets in every family; fantasies and myths that, without being properly comprehended, nevertheless have the power to affect the lives of each member.

It had been understood by the Maynards, that Georgina was to be the one who would make her parents proud. She had always been beautiful; the photograph albums proved that, turn the pages and see how the chubby, laughing baby grew into the pretty, smiling schoolgirl. It had all been recorded. Georgina in ski-clothes, in ballgown, on horse-back. Ruth's little sister, clinging charmingly to the arm of some equally charismatic young man.

Ruth's unreal childhood was also preserved in the photo-graph album. A gawky, solemn child; she had stood with knees bent, chest concave. Her long dark hair tied in two wispy plaits, her stooped shoulders already, at the age of thirteen, conveying an apologetic attitude of mind. She had loved Georgina. Loved the coral lips, the speedwell eyes, and the dense blonde hair that rippled on her little sister's shoulders. Being close to Georgina had been comparable with owning the sunshine; until Gina at the age of eighteen went away to study drama, and Love had walked out of The Mullions on slender adventurous feet; never to return.

George Maynard had begun to die very slowly, some years before his actual departure; and Harry, who had stoutly declined the offer of a brand new house as a wedding present, became pleasantly aware of the sick man's dependence on him. In time, Ruth had been persuaded to resign her job and stay at home to nurse her father through his last illness; and her mother no longer complained of the smell of antiseptic: or insisted on the necessity of Chanel No 5.

Harry Flemming soon grew plump and sleek at her father's table. He became the man of the house. Ran the factory single-handed; played bridge with her mother, gave orders to the gardener; stayed overnight in London, on urgent business. Or so he said. Every day, they had moved one step further away from one another. They both talked, but only listened to their own voices. She was outside of the mainstream of Harry's life; isolated in her father's sickroom.

In those days Ruth was often aware of her own shortcomings, without ever quite knowing what she should do about them. When her husband's waning interest in her became so marked that she could no longer attribute it to lack of opportunity, she began to visit expensive little boutiques, in search of the gauzy creations that looked so fetching on Georgina. The results of these disastrous forays, still hung at the back of her wardrobe, several years later.

Her father had died, as he had lived. Slipping away on a bitter November night, very quietly, and giving the minimum of trouble.

The wording of her father's Will had been bizarre and disconcerting. It was bound to have set in motion certain thoughts that would lead her to strange destinations. 'To my beloved elder daughter, Ruth Alice Flemming, I leave my entire estate, so that she may, before it is too late, experience freedom.'

Her mother had hinted that pressure must have been brought to bear, in those long night-watches in the sickroom. Not that she cared for her own sake; she had never, she declared, been dependent upon George Maynard for money, or anything else. Oh no! It was the slight to Georgina that had rankled, and caused Mrs Maynard to fume and rage. Ruth had offered to share with her sister; but Georgina, unbearably distant and cold, had declined, politely. Ruth's mother, who said she had always wanted to travel, departed for Italy with one of her bridge-playing friends, leaving Ruth alone at last with the silent, deferential Harry. It had been at this point in her life, that questions began to stir in her mind about her husband, and the marriage that was not a marriage. She began to think about love; it was never spoken of in her family. Love, it had been hinted, might warp the judgement, and cloud issues. It might even be considered a weakness. She wondered if Harry could grow to love her, and if she would recognise such a gift if he should ever offer it to her. She knew that he loved the house and its contents; she had watched him trace every hallmark on each prized piece of antique silver. She had grown up in this houseful of treasures. Among chairs too valuable to sit on, among books too expensive to leaf through. Ruth had learned early on to be wary of all that she handled – especially people.

If only she could have run to Harry Flemming in those days, thrown her arms around him, pleaded for his understanding. But she could not. Love whispered inside her mind and provided an answer. A child was what she needed. A miniature Ruth on whom she could lavish all her stored-up love and affection.

It had already occurred to her that a man as cool and respectful as Harry, might just possibly be incapable of successful impregnation. But she lacked the courage to put this suspicion to the test. Instead she bought time in an infertility clinic, where she was measured, prodded and tested, without any positive conclusion. Everything about her, they said, was a contra-indication. Her age, her rundown physical condition: the mood of depression that had set in since her father's death. At night she would sit by the window and watch the lights come on in the Hillcrest district. She had imagined the scenes in those neat little bungalows and houses. The scatter of toys, the tiny garments to be washed and ironed; the young mothers lifting their babies for the last feed and change. She had looked at her own ordered household, and longed for a cot in the corner of the bedroom, a bucketful of nappies in soak in the bathroom, and a pram to block up her dove-grey hallway.

She still grieved for her father; this man, with whom she had lived for most of her life, but never really known. It was ironic that she should only have begun to love and understand him through the extraordinary wording of his Will. She wondered what her father had known about Harry; or Georgina, for that matter. She had never considered him to be a vindictive man; and yet the terms of his Will seemed to her to be unnecessarily divisive.

Ruth had an overpowering urge at that time to substitute new life for old death. But Harry either would not, or could not, co-operate with her. He was only concerned with stamping his mark on the house. He began to lay up treasure for himself; he bought modern paintings and *objets d'art*, just as if they were not cluttered up to the ceilings with such bric-a-brac already.

His conversation, never stimulating, became almost mono-syllabic. A dull breakfast-chant about shareholders meetings, possible strike-action and an alarming recession in the hosiery business. He invited Ruth to take some interest in such matters; after all, Harry said, it was really her factory. There were so many things she could have done in that spring and summer. She could have fostered a baby, or tried for adoption. Or become a business tycoon.

Instead, she took to haunting those parts of the city where the mothers tended to congregate with their young children. She had stood, tall and awkward, among prams and push-chairs in recreation areas and at school gates. She would sit for hours on park benches, ostensibly feeding the pigeons. After a time, since her presence had not yet been challenged, Ruth grew more daring. She began to visit, and mingle with the young mothers in baby-clinics, willing some overbur-dened mother to hand her an infant to mind; and, of course, in the end – it happened.

She had found the clinic on a housing estate just beyond the city. It was a pleasant one-storey building of new red-brick, and set among grass and flowers. The path that led up to the double swing-doors was bordered with marigolds and blue and white lobelia. The sun shone out of a clear blue sky that day, and bees hummed among the flowers. Ruth never ceased to be surprised, in later years, at the ease with which she had entered such places. Perhaps her severely dressed hair and navy-blue suit gave a false impression. No one ever chal-lenged her presence, even though she so obviously lacked the obligatory baby. On this particular occasion she was handed a cup of tea and a digestive biscuit as she walked in the door.

The young mother was in her early twenties; a slim blonde girl with long sweeps of hair hanging loose on her shoulders.

She wore a sprigged cotton sundress, and her arms and legs were tanned a deep brown. Ruth had watched her come through the heavy swing-doors, a small yelling child on each hand.

'Can you help me?' she asked, 'it's the baby. I've left him outside in the porch. It's so noisy in here.' She looked down at the wailing toddlers. 'The twins are due for their jabs today. But if I bring the baby inside he'll be sure to wake up – and then I'll have all three of them crying.' She paused, and breathed deeply. 'I don't like to leave him alone. You hear such funny stories, don't you?'

Ruth agreed that, indeed, there were some very odd people about, and that it was impossible for a mother to be too careful. She congratulated the girl on her sound common-sense, and moved out to the porch in a dream. He lay on a clean white sheet, eyes tightly closed, small chest heaving gently beneath the blue nylon romper. His rounded limbs were gold from the sun, and his soft damp hair stood out in little dark points all around his head.

Ruth had started to tremble.

The porch was secluded; the Mini was parked out of sight, just around the corner. She lifted him gently, and felt suddenly weak at the fresh sweet baby smell that came with him.

She had taken three steps away from the pram when the doors burst open, and the girl in the sundress was back, swinging fast through the clinic entrance.

'I thought you worked here,' she accused, 'I thought you were one of the helpers!'

'A bee,' Ruth had improvised glibly, 'it flew under the hood of the pram. I was afraid it might sting him.' She relinquished the baby, at once, and made sure that she handed him over with the air of a woman who did not much care for the burden of small damp infants.

The girl's face cleared slightly. 'Thanks, anyway,' she said uncertainly, 'it was good of you to take the trouble.' She backed away through the heavy swing doors, the baby clutched tight to her heart. As she went, she called doubtfully over her shoulder, 'Thanks – anyway.'

Ruth walked away down the narrow paving; past the blurred blue and white of the lobelia, and the clumps of orange. It had been a close call. She had meant to steal him.

She went back to the Mini and slumped in the hot leather seat. She studied the procession of mothers and prams going into the clinic. Ruth knew then that it would only be a matter of time before she leaned over another unguarded pram, and walked off with another woman's baby.

## 6.

Mrs Hardy was a regular visitor to Mainstay. She sat in the yellow chair, hands folded, eyes downcast. She knew, had known since her very first visit, that any help Ruth might offer would be swiftly refused; and yet, once every fortnight, they went through the same motions. She talked. Ruth listened. Now and again Ruth inserted a sympathetic murmur. Mrs Hardy's eyes brimmed with tears. Over the years she had exhibited several black eyes, broken fingers, cracked ribs, and a variety of cuts and bruises.

Jack Hardy was a jovial fellow, the life and soul of The Bird in Hand. A regular eight-pints-a-night man; he never attacked when mellow. Mr Hardy only struck out in moments of stone-cold sobriety. Or so his wife said.

They lived in a small terraced house down in Tulip Fields. Mrs Hardy did her best with the damp little cottage. Her curtains hung in neat folds behind well polished windows. Jack did his share. He conscientiously painted the house in chocolate and cream every other year. The small, sour patch of front garden was regularly coaxed, to produce a mass of old-fashioned flowers. Jack refused to move out of St Joseph's. He was born and grew up there. The dark little house had belonged to his mother; he belonged in it.

Mrs Hardy wished to leave St Joseph's: she longed, desperately, to live in a brand-new house with picture-windows, central-heating, and a shaven lawn with rosebushes round it. If she would only bide her time, Ruth consoled her, the demolition crews and their bulldozers would make all her dreams come true.

Meanwhile, Jack Hardy was not to be shifted: and his wife declined to leave, or file any complaint against him. Even today, through split and puffy lips, she reiterated her intention of 'sticking it out to the bitter end'.

They had no children. Not her choice, she insisted. Things just never worked out the way she had planned them.

After the incident in the baby clinic, Ruth had deliberately avoided all areas of the city that might offer temptation. She replanned her father's garden that autumn: built a rockery, and a pool with a fountain. She hadn't really worried about her depression; if she considered it at all, it was to console herself with the thought that a certain amount of misery was to be expected. With her father dead, her mother globe-trotting, and Georgina still declining all offers to visit, it was hardly surprising that she, the daughter who had never left home, was finding so keen an adjustment a little difficult to handle.

There was also Harry. His trips to London had become more frequent and of longer duration. He would come back to The Mullions bringing her boxes of handmade chocolates; and smelling of sex and Arpège. Oh, he did his duty by her on a Sunday morning; after he'd drunk his early-morning tea and swallowed a few aspirin tablets – and before going off to play golf. But she had also found time to notice just lately how often his eyes followed other women, and she wondered how she could ever have imagined that Harry Flemming was a cold man.

Ruth had drifted about the city that autumn, gazing into babywear shop windows: every pavement and café seemed crowded with serene young women who wore flowered maternity smocks, and looked as if they alone held the mystery and magic of life inside them. At the end of November she tried to tell Harry about her obsession; but he either failed to grasp the significance of what she was saying, or defended himself by being purposely obtuse.

Three weeks before Christmas, and there was an influx of tiny, excited children into the city centre. The main streets were hung with coloured lights, and Santa Claus grottos appeared in all the big stores.

Ruth hung a rear bedroom with nursery-rhyme wallpaper, and had the floor close-fitted with a washable carpet. She went shopping. She purchased a white wicker rocking cradle, a baby bath, nappy buckets; and a selection of garments suitable for an age range of birth to six months. She also laid in a large stock of baby food, feeding bottles, and sterilising equipment. Ruth had been busy. For the first time since her father's death, she was making a definite move: she felt cheerful, hummed softly to herself. She never considered how this mythical child was to be acquired. For the moment, at least, she had been more than content to watch, and await her opportunity.

The girl had parked the pram in the supermarket doorway, in full view of every customer who entered the store. Ruth had lately become a connoisseur of prams, and this one was in the luxury bracket, although it seemed an unlikely appendage for this girl, who wore stained denim jeans, and a baggy green sweater. Ruth kept her in view as she sauntered away, wire basket in hand, down the crowded aisles. She stood close to the girl as the improbable mop of orange hair hovered over the ice-cream cabinets, brushed up against the display of potato crisps, and was finally pushed from her eyes while she made her selection of chocolate bars. The girl's fingers were ringless, but Ruth had known, without any doubt, that the baby was hers.

She followed her out through the checkpoint. The high white pram made an easy target to track, for in spite of the cold, the girl walked slowly; she pushed the child with an absentminded air. The pram and its fittings were new and expensive. Several passers-by spared second glances for the pink satin coverlet and lacy pillow, and the chime of silver bells carefully pinned just inside the hood. It was neary dusk, but the Christmas streets had been brilliant with neon set-pieces, and a million tinsel stars. For once, Ruth's height had proved an advantage; it allowed her to keep the amazing orange head in view without coming too close.

The girl loitered her way through the city centre; occasion-ally she halted to gaze into shop windows. All at once she made a swift and unexpected detour through a fruit and vegetable market, and into a maze of dark alleyways. Ruth thought she had lost her; and then she heard the tinkling of bells, and knew that the pram must be somewhere close by. She turned a corner just in time to see the girl wedge her pram up against a plate-glass window, in between a carelessly propped bicycle, and a push-chair piled high with firewood. Without stopping to apply the brake, the girl had strolled into the sleazy café, and abandoned the baby without a backward glance.

Ruth began to tremble, as she had on that earlier occasion in the porch of the baby clinic. She held fast to the thought of the nursery she had prepared. The rocking-cradle and its yellow sheets and blankets; the teddy-bear and Raggedy-Ann doll seated on the window-sill; the brightly coloured mobiles hanging from the ceiling. The girl would be sad for a week or two. Perhaps she would make one of those dramatic television appeals for the return of her baby. But she was very young; there would be plenty of years for her, in which she might yet get married and have other children.

Ruth moved into the mouth of an alleyway, and caught her breath. She felt threatened by the quality of the darkness in these run down, badly lit streets. This was no respectable, tree-lined avenue up in Hillcrest. This, she now realised, was the far edge of St Joseph's; a district that was notorious and to be avoided; and yet fear only sharpened her sense of the dramatic. The incident in the baby clinic had been no more than a practice run for this, the real action. She was out, and on the move at last. Even as she watched and waited, the first ominous snowflakes of winter had caught and melted on her lips and eyebrows.

The café had been a regular comfort-stop for long-distance lorry drivers. A patch of uneven ground at one side of the building was crowded with high sided vehicles and loaded trailers. She was forced to postpone her move to the opposite side of the road, while a heavy-set man in a reefer jacket walked along to the patch of waste-ground and climbed up to the cab of his Bedford lorry.

She had taken one step off the kerb and towards the pram, when the door of the café swung outwards. Blue denim writhed and grappled with black leather as the fighting, shouting youths rolled across the pavement and into the gutter. She saw a badly aimed boot strike the propped-up bike, which at once began a slow and inevitable slide along the café window to dislodge the unbraked pram and the laden pushchair. At the same moment, the engine of the Bedford spluttered, caught, and finally turned over.

Ruth had screamed as the high white pram rode majestically over the kerbstone, straight into the path of the oncoming lorry. The sound was mixed up with the screeching of brakes, and the wail of a very young baby. She flung herself forwards, grabbed a handful of warm damp wool, and fell backwards.

Down in the gutter she had cradled her prize, and wept for a moment from shock. Light from the café window fell across the baby's face, it looked up at her with grave, wide open eyes and suddenly stopped crying. Ruth found herself concentrating quite fiercely on small unimportant details. The pink jacket and bonnet had been hand-knitted in a lacy elaborate pattern. There were rosebuds embroidered upon them in white and yellow silks: and an inch of frilly pink dress hung below the jacket. Some woman, a grandmother perhaps, had already loved and cherished this child, and prepared for her coming.

Ruth could not bear to look at the mass of flattened metal that had once been an elegant pram. Amazingly, the silver bells had remained untouched. They still hung from the twisted hood, and chimed softly on the cold night air.

Suddenly, she had been surrounded by people. The driver of the lorry was pale, and very angry. Two policemen appeared, but the youths who had caused the near tragedy had long since vanished down the maze of dark alleys. The proprietor of the café brought soup and a blanket. He said that Ruth had saved Samantha's life, and that rotten little bitch Sharon should also be down in the gutter with her baby – being grateful, instead of having screaming hysterics in his back room. After all, he said, her mum had worked all hours to buy that pram, and now look at it! Better all round, he snorted, if they'd had the kid adopted.

Ruth had looked down at the soft pink mound underneath the blanket, Samantha? Oh no. Her baby was to have been called Victoria: and naming the girl with the orange hair was no part of the game she'd played, either. She glared at the policeman. 'It's all spoiled,' she lamented, 'this is not what I intended.'

'Don't worry about that pram,' he said, 'prams can be replaced a damn sight quicker than babies.'

She had refused the offer of hospital treatment; and the high white ambulance, shockingly reminiscent of the ruined pram had gathered up the girl called Sharon, and the baby called Samantha, and charmed them away down the snowy street. The staff from the café returned to their counters; the lorry driver, having shown his papers, was allowed to continue his journey. A policeman requested that she should attend at the local Bridewell on the following morning to sign a statement.

Georgina was hardly equipped to fill the role into which Ruth had now cast her. But there had been no one else. 'I don't understand you,' she'd snapped, 'you have the money, the factory, the house – what more can you want?'

'I think – I think I must be ill,' murmured Ruth, 'I have this – this compulsion to – to do odd things.'

'What kind of odd things?'

Ruth could not bring herself to describe her aberrations: it would have sounded too bizarre. Instead, she'd taken Georgina upstairs and showed her the pale yellow nursery.

'But, darling,' said her sister suspiciously, 'you don't have a baby.'

'I know,' wept Ruth, 'that's the trouble.'

'Well, adopt one, or something, if you feel that passionately about it.' She'd looked at Ruth keenly. 'You're not thinking of going in for the odd bit of kidnapping are you?'

'Of course not,' lied Ruth, 'don't be stupid. It's all Harry's fault. He might take to a child of his own, but he doesn't seem too keen on adoption.'

'Rubbish,' said Georgina, 'it's your house. Your money. Put your foot down.'

'That's the other half of the problem,' Ruth muttered. But nobody heard her.

Later that evening, Georgina, who was honestly trying to help had said vaguely, 'Why don't you try volunteer work – you know – Meals on Wheels, War on Want shops? Keep yourself busy, Ruthie. Don't brood. They say that some women can only conceive once they've stopped worrying about it.'

'But you've always made fun of charity workers,' said Ruth. 'You once called them the "twin-set and pearls brigade". You once said it would be better to die of starvation that to eat those awful dried-up dinners from the WVS.'

'I couldn't have said that,' cried Georgina. 'I don't know anything about it.' When she lied, she was brazen about it. 'Remember those stories father used to tell,' she went on persuasively, 'about grandmother riding out in her carriage to take broth to the poor.'

Ruth frowned. 'I always thought that sounded so patronising: and anyway, it all happened back in the 1870s.'

'Same principles apply, darling: and surely anything's worth a try in your condition.'

The policeman who took her statement on the following morning had looked sideways at her watch and rings, her expensive handbag and shoes. 'And what brought you into St Joseph's after dark, on a night like that?' he asked her.

'I was shopping,' Ruth lied, 'looking for a Christmas Tree. I discovered that big fruit and vegetable market – you know the one I mean?' He nodded. 'Well, then I got lost in those long dark alleyways, and emerged to find myself opposite the café.' She laughed then, on a high artificial note quite unlike herself.

'Lucky for Sharon that you did,' said the policeman.

'What will happen to them, the girl and the baby?'

'Nothing much, ma'am. Nobody got hurt, thanks to you. We've had a word, but I don't see it making much difference. Irresponsible y'see. That's the trouble with Sharon; accident-prone I suppose you could call it.'

'I was wondering,' Ruth said diffidently, 'if you could give me her address. I would really like to help her –'

'Best not,' the policeman interrupted, 'they're a pretty rough family. Sharon's dad's doing time in Walton for GBH – grievous bodily harm. You could find yourself landed in all sorts of problems if you got involved with that lot. No,' he said comfortably, 'better leave 'em to Mainstay. They know what they're doing with families like the Spencers.'

'Mainstay?'

'A volunteer group,' he explained briefly, 'ladies like yourself, ma'am. They've set themselves up in a house round the corner. Spent money on it too. They're a bit like the Sally-Army,' he grinned, 'but without the religion and the bonnets.'

Her involvement with the group called Mainstay had begun three weeks later. Her nursing qualifications, and the fact that she owned a car and was willing to spend part of each day in St Joseph's, had ensured her of instant entry into their organisation.

Imperceptibly, her depression had lightened. Piece by piece, she'd dismantled the yellow nursery and distributed the luxury items among hard-pressed mothers; which had earned her the instant and lasting reputation of being a soft-touch.

If Harry Flemming had ever known about that rear bedroom, and his wife's obsession with maternal urges, he gave no sign. He had accepted the news of Ruth's recruitment to Mainstay with polite relief; after all, her absorption with families in trouble made her easier to handle. Tensions eased between them. Ruth, busy and concerned had hardly noticed the signs of his incipient defection, six years later.

*Part Two*

# SPRING

# 1.

A deceptive mildness in the air. A blackened church spire stabbed a watered-silk sky; and spring shuffled sideways into the city.

It came rolling across the cobblestones in St Joseph's market packed in cartons and crates. It nodded from chipped plastic buckets filled with sleek green daffodil buds; nestled in tissue-lined boxes where jewel-red tulips were packed tightly together. Spring. That old deceiver. That cure-all.

The bud-vase on Ruth Flemming's desk held a spray of mauve freesia. The scent, in the over-heated office was more potent than cannabis resin. Held more visions than lysergic acid. Gave more ease to the mind than Valium or Librium.

People hurt in springtime. Numbed sensibilities were coming to life in the warm April weather, and her clients were beginning to count up their winter bruises. Ruth, too, had the odd nick and gash of her own that cried out for attention. For these were the days when the middle-aged woman looked into her mirror, and remembered how trusting and hopeful she had been at sixteen.

Ruth slotted the Mini in between two parked patrol cars, and

39

wondered which family in Nelson Street was receiving police attention. She knocked at Number Twelve.

'Come you in, Mrs Flemming,' lilted Billy Evans, 'we got some company this morning.'

Della Smith lounged in one armchair, and a constable called Parsons sat stiffly in the other. Billy Evans resumed what had obviously been his previous position, leaning nonchalantly up against the wall. Dominating the little set-piece, in every sense of the word, was Detective Sergeant McInnes. He stood with his extra-long spine turned towards the fire; effectively shutting off all warmth from the rest of the room.

'Whatever's going on here?' Ruth snapped, unwisely.

'Nothing that need concern you – my dear lady!' sneered Detective McInnes. 'A little matter of a stolen wallet. It's just between us and this-er-lady.'

Delilah Smith drew up a mouthful of saliva and aimed it accurately at McInnes's left shoe. Ruth saw the policeman flinch and clench his fist. The constable snapped the elastic band around his notebook and stood up. McInnes addressed himself to Billy. 'Don't forget – I've got my eye on you, Evans. I don't like the company you're keeping.' The policeman raised two ironic fingers to his right eyebrow and aimed his next shot at Ruth. 'Watch out for these two love-birds won't you madam? Between them they've already made a proper monkey of you.'

As the front door closed behind the two policemen, Ruth selected Billy Evans as her first target. 'What are you doing here, Billy?'

'I lives here now, Mrs Flemming.'

'I'm amazed to hear that.'

'He can live where he bloody well wants to – he don' need your say-so.' Della Smith, severely hung-over that morning, and already harassed by the law, was in an uncompromising mood.

Ruth ignored her.

'Billy,' she asked, 'what about your room in the Hostel?'

He looked uneasy. He knew how much difficulty she had experienced in placing him there. He shuffled his feet together in a strange little dance.

'Well, I give it up, a few days ago, ma'am.' He looked fondly at Della. 'She really do need me, Mrs Flemming; you can see that, can't you?'

'But do you need her? Look, you've kept out of trouble for almost a year now. But a few days in Della's company, and what happens? You've got McInnes coming after you again – now is it worth it?'

Billy indicated Della. 'She's done nothing; honest ma'am. Some fella swore she pinched his wallet.'

'Did you Della?'

'Do I look like somebody what's got a hundred quid?'

'That's a new dress you're wearing.'

'Billy bought it for me. Anyway – that's none o' your bloody business. I don' always have to wear them rags what come out of your old poor-bag.'

'The bedrooms in this house are unusable,' Ruth warned them, 'so where are you sleeping, Billy?'

Della caught her meaning. 'It's all decent,' she shouted, 'he brung his own bed with him. He's in the front room, by his self. He don' come in here wi' me and my Paisley.' As Ruth continued to look doubtingly at her, she continued, 'Go an' look fer yerself, you suspicious old cow, if you don' believe me!'

'And what will happen to Paisley in this new arrangement?' Ruth asked coldly. 'Are you planning to leave her alone in the house while you and Billy are off on a drinking session?'

Della's thin little face lit up with malicious pleasure. 'Got you there, my lady! My Paisley goes back to the vans' at the week-end. She stops wi' my Gran from Friday to Sunday.'

'I didn't know that your people were still in the area, Della.'

'They watches me all the time. Jus' like you do, missus. They want Paisley back; but they dursn't go agen' the Social people. My Gran don' give up all that easy. She'll get Paisley off me, if she can. Then they'll move on: wi'out me.'

# 2.

April sunshine sought out the grubby terrazzo of her kitchen floor, and the unwashed dishes in the sink. In the rest of the house there was evidence of Ruth's neglect. Dust lay on every surface, and the silver had tarnished to gold from her inattention. Out in the garden, snowdrops and crocus had bloomed and died, unseen.

There was still no word from Harry. A letter came from her mother. Mrs Maynard had rented a flat in Rome, and intended to stay there. Phone calls, from a man called Clive Jessop, at the factory grew increasingly urgent in tone. There were certain grave problems, he said. Mr Flemming's decision was needed on matters of extreme importance. How much longer, asked Jessop, did Harry intend to remain in New York? Queries from the Bank, he informed her, were getting increasingly difficult to deal with: and so what did Mrs Flemming propose to do about it?

The manager of her local branch was a fussy, middle-aged man called Hipgood. He glanced irritably at his watch, and then wasted time shifting papers from one side of his desk to the other. He sighed with the air of a man who was about to be asked to move mountains.

'The Bank has written to you several times since January, Mrs Flemming.'

'I know, Mr Hipgood, I'm sorry. I've had a few problems, just lately.'

He looked at her consideringly. 'Ye-es,' he said, 'you have, haven't you?'

So, she thought, they were already gossiping up at the Golf Club.

'My husband,' she said firmly, 'deals with all financial matters.'

Hipgood leaned back in his armchair and steepled his fingers. 'Ah, yes. Your husband. Where precisely is he?'

The question found her ridiculously unprepared. She began to stammer. 'My – my husband's whereabouts are hardly any business of yours, Mr Hipgood –'

'But I'm afraid they are, my dear lady.' He looked severe. 'Are you aware that the Receiver is about to be called in at George Maynard's; and, of course,' he breathed deeply, 'there is still the outstanding matter of the loan.'

She had never given much thought to money. Had never needed to. Even when Harry had said, 'Look, Ruth – we've got a bit of a cash-flow problem at the factory, I think we might need to raise some money – with The Mullions as surety.' Even then, she had not really worried about it. She had agreed, as he had known she would. Signed the necessary papers, and pretended that her grasp of matters concerning liquidity and assets was as keen as his own. She had not really cared.

'But that loan was supposed to save the business,' she told Hipgood, 'and now you're talking about the Receiver being brought in.'

The bank manager looked down at his blotter, and would not meet her gaze. 'Next Monday, I'm afraid, Mrs Flemming. There is nothing I can do to halt it.'

'But the money,' cried Ruth, 'what happened to the money we raised on the house?'

He cleared his throat, noisily. 'I'm afraid you've been far too trusting. I can't be absolutely certain, at this point, but I suspect that very little of that loan has found its way into the factory. Enough ready cash was left in the account to see matters through for about three months. But your husband made several large withdrawals before he left for New York –'

But he didn't go to New York, she wanted to shout. He took the poacher and the egg-timer with him. He's probably nursing an imaginary stomach-ulcer in some picturesque cottage in the country.

She said: 'I had no reason not to trust him. My father always relied on him completely.' Ruth held on to the seat of her chair to steady herself. 'What exactly is my position now, Mr Hipgood?'

'It means,' he said gently, 'that you owe the bank eighty thousand pounds, plus interest. I'm truly sorry, my dear. But you can see that I had to clarify the position.'

'Let me think it over.'

'But of course. Talk it over with the rest of the family – and contact me again – on Monday morning.'

There was nothing to talk over: and no family with whom she might do so. On Monday morning Ruth telephoned Mr Hipgood. 'I shall be vacating The Mullions on the first of May,' she told him. 'You have my solicitor's name and address. Please refer all matters concerning my husband and the business to him in the future.'

## 3.

The oldest gravestones in the churchyard dated back to the early seventeen hundreds. The whole area of St Joseph's had once been a village surrounded by farmsteads. The place names confirmed this. Lark Hill, Miller's Lane, Ladysmock Gardens, Tulip Fields.

Over the years a small square of cottages and places of business had crept up to, and surrounded the church. There was a blacksmith's shop where the few dray horses still used by the city brewers came regularly to be shod. The Bird in Hand pub stood on one corner, and a small junk-and-curio shop on another. The antique shops that formed one side of the square were much older than much of the merchandise that filled their windows. The flower-shop, and Dino's Italian café with their red and white striped awnings, were more recent additions. Tucked away in a corner, over-shadowed by the church, was Friar's Walk, and old Mrs Pomeroy's cottage.

For the past six months Number Seven Friar's Walk had been one of Ruth Flemming's regular Friday morning calls. Mrs Pomeroy lived there, alone, since the death of her husband; an old lady at risk, who refused to move out to a council flat in a concrete tower-block. Ruth collected her pension and did any heavy shopping; on her return there was always a cup of strong tea waiting for her, and a plate of home-made biscuits.

On this Friday morning, there was no answer when she called. She rapped several times on the heavy iron knocker, dislodging huge flakes of the dry brown paint as she did so. The small sash-window that faced the square was hung with close, screening nets which made it impossible for her to see into the little front room. She began to feel apprehensive. The incidence of violent crime in the district was growing. A missing person in this area of the city, was more readily presumed by his neighbours to have been mugged or murdered, than to have suffered a mishap from natural or accidental causes.

Across at the flower-shop a girl called Mandy was setting out buckets full of tulips and narcissi all along the shop-front: making the pavement bloom, in flagrant contravention of the local bye-laws. The blinds were still down in the classier antique shops, and the curtains close drawn across the Bird in Hand's windows.

Mario, son of Dino, was hosing away cigarette ends and rubbish from the front of the café. So clean, this Italian family, thought Ruth. Always swilling and brooming.

From the open door of the dark little junk-and-curio shop, Mrs Mandelbaum watched the square. A heavy, slow-moving woman, she seemed always to know what went on in the district without needing to move from behind her old wooden counter. 'Mrs Pomeroy? Why, she was took off in an ambulance, dearie. Soon after seven this morning. Milkman found her. Collapsed on her kitchen floor. You shouldn't never have left her there, Mrs Flemming. Not at her age.'

'You don't know which hospital –?'

'Be the City General, dearie. Like I said to my Manny, we shan't be seeing old Mrs Pomeroy back here again.'

Ruth arrived at the City General Hospital twenty minutes later. A young Asian doctor told her that her client had died soon after admission. A massive stroke, he said, a hopeless case. But at that advanced age it was to be expected. She listened with only a part of her mind. There were arrangements to be made. A son who lived in Scotland must be found and informed. The daughter, who lived in St Joseph's, but never visited, would have to be notified of her mother's passing.

Ruth knew she would always remember this particular old lady. Spare and erect in a flowered-print dress and white apron, she had regularly swept last autumn's leaves from the porches of St Joseph's church. Mrs Pomeroy had taken a pride in maintaining her standards. Without the aid of a washing-machine or a vacuum cleaner; lacking bathroom and inside lavatory, her faith in carbolic soap and elbow-grease had enabled her to survive, sweet and clean, in an age that demanded instant convenience and material abundance.

It was already mid-afternoon when Ruth returned to the Mainstay building. She had found the events of that morning unexpectedly distressing. There were so few people in her life whom she could call 'friend', that the loss of this one frail contact would leave her feeling colder; more exposed. She listened, absent-mindedly, to discussions between her colleagues of their respective visits. Sharp exchanges were made, in which she took no part. She reported, very briefly, on the death of her client; and then went on to explain, in great detail, the new domestic arrangements at present in force, in Number Twelve Nelson street. It was decided by Imogen Hirst that very little could or should be done about Della Smith at that juncture. But a sharp eye on Paisley's welfare, it was agreed, must always be Ruth's main priority when dealing with this family.

The church clock struck seven as she left the Mainstay building. Down in the car park she met Sam Bright who had also worked late. 'You look whacked, Ruth. Heavy day?'

'Mrs Pomeroy of Seven Friar's Walk died this morning.'

'Sorry. I'd forgotten about that.' He hesitated. 'I'm on my way round to the Bird in Hand, care to join me?'

Her instinct was to refuse, and then she remembered her empty house, and pocketed her car keys. She fell into step beside him. Away from the office, Ruth and Sam were awkward with one another. They sat at a table well away from the bar, and made small-talk. Sam Bright was a smiling Jamaican who worked mainly with the large immigrant population of St Joseph's. He was obviously well-known to the clientèle of the Bird in Hand.

Ruth noticed how readily he was grinned at, and greeted by them, with a familiarity which she found almost enviable.

Sam was not so relaxed in her company. A strained silence fell between them. He swirled the remains of the drink in his glass, and gazed into the whirlpool. 'You in some kinda trouble, Ruth?'

'It's been a bad day, Sam.'

'More than that, gal! I believe it's more than that.'

The table between them was narrow: glass-topped, wet with beer-stains. But she was suddenly tempted to push all her problems across it. Sam had just called her 'gal' with a warmth that made her eyes sting.

Secretly she had always believed that there must be something very wrong with a woman to whom bad things happened. Because of this rooted conviction she now found it hard to confide her troubles.

She selected the most recent of her problems as being the least revealing. 'From the end of the month I have nowhere to live.'

His brown face creased in disbelief. 'You can't mean that?'

'I'm afraid I do.'

'But – but you're married to a rich man. You live in that damned great house up in Hillcrest. Everybody knows that you only work down in St Joseph's to –'

'To pass away time, Sam?'

His dark eyes glittered. 'Excuse me. I only repeat what I hear.'

He banged down his glass on the table. 'You know something? You're a pretty hard person to talk to.'

'Well – I'm sorry.'

Sam leaned forwards. 'I was watching you, this afternoon, up in Imogen's room. You cared about that old woman who died, didn't you? You care about all of them. But who in hell cares about you, Ruth Flemming? Not your lousy clients!' He made an impatient gesture, 'We spend most of our working hours among people in trouble, and at the end of the day the majority of them don't give a damn what we do, one way or the other. We're just another rotten thorn in their suffering flesh.'

'No Sam. I can't believe that!'

'Then you'd better believe it Ruth; because that's how it is.' He leaned towards her, across the table. 'You've got to keep something inside you intact. Hold onto some strength for yourself.' He grinned and relaxed. 'You know something? I think you're a bloody nice lady.'

Ruth blushed. 'You don't really know me.'

'I know more than you think. Word gets around. People talk.'

'What sort of talk?'

'That you spend your own money on clients.'

'Don't we all, at some time or another?'

'It happens – yes. But you worry about them; on your own private time.'

'Don't you, Sam?'

'Not in the same way that you do. It's not good, Ruth. Believe me!'

Sam's unexpected concern overwhelmed her; and she saw the amazing pink pearl of his fingernails through a blur of tears. She looked down at the brown left hand that was covering hers. 'Sorry Sam. I only ever cry when I'm drunk.'

'On one dry Martini? Look Ruth: we've all noticed it lately. Something seriously wrong with you, isn't there? Why won't you let somebody help you?'

'It's a long story,' she said, 'long and boring. My only real concern at this moment, is with finding somewhere suitable to live.'

He sighed. Sam Bright, she suspected, was as capable as the next man of putting two and two together.

'No more husband, Ruth?'

'No more husband, Sam.'


On an April evening, masked by twilight, St Joseph's square looked old and safe. They strolled back to the Mainstay car park by way of Friar's Walk.

'Did the old lady own the house?' asked Sam.

'No. It belongs to the Church. She once told me all about it. It seems that the rent is a nominal one on condition that the tenant will scrub the church steps every week-end, and sweep out the porches.'

He laughed, 'Could you do that?'

'Scrub the church steps? Well, yes. I suppose so. If I had to.'

'Then go do it, gal!'

Ruth stopped walking and faced him. 'Live here do you

mean, in this cottage?'

He shrugged. 'Bit of a come-down for you, of course, after living all your life up in Hillcrest. Depends on how desperate you really are.'

'Oh – I'm desperate.'

'Then do it Ruth. Don't waste any time though. Go and see Canon Flint in the morning.'

Her appointment with the Canon of St Joseph's was at ten that Saturday morning. As she crossed the square a furniture van pulled away from Seven Friar's Walk. The daughter, who had rarely found time to visit the house in her mother's lifetime, had obviously lost no time in claiming the contents.

'So you're interested in the cottage?' asked the Canon. 'Had you a suitable tenant in mind?'

'Myself – Canon.'

'You?' He sounded so surprised that Ruth could only conclude that he too had heard the rumour that she was some kind of Woolworth heiress.

'My husband has left me,' she said flatly. 'He mortgaged the house that I live in, and then reneged on the debt. From the first day of May I shall be homeless.'

The Canon looked grave. 'I'm sorry to hear that. Are you quite sure there's no chance –?'

'He left on the fourth of January; today is the nineteenth of April. There has been no word from him in that time.'

'Are you totally without funds?'

Ruth smiled at the clergyman's phrasing. It was precisely the question she herself often put to a hard-up client.

'No,' she reassured him, 'I have a small annuity that my grandmother left me.'

He was thoughtful. 'It's very dilapidated, you know. There's no bathroom.'

'I can do any necessary repairs,' she insisted, 'I'll pay you a reasonable rent. I'll even fulfil the conditions.'

'Conditions?'

'Of the tenancy. Cleaning the church steps and the porches.'

He laughed. 'That won't be required, Mrs Flemming. Not in your case.'

'But I want to.'

He opened a drawer in his desk and lifted out an ancient

49

brass key. 'Here you are then. Shall we say thirty pounds, paid calendar monthly, and the occasional brush and dust up in the church porches – if your conscience demands it.'

Without Mrs Pomeroy's broom to halt it, the dust and waste paper had already crept up to and blocked the doorway of Seven Friar's Walk. Inside the cottage, a scent of lavender and carbolic soap overlay the soot in the city air.

Ruth now realised, that in six months of regular Friday morning visits, she had never stepped further than the old lady's kitchen.

Now, she walked through the house and discovered with pleasure that the ceilings were low and open-beamed; and because the house stood on varying levels, little steps led up into some rooms, and down into others. It was a tiny house, built by unpretentious men who had used wood and stone for their qualities of durability rather than effect. It consisted of two bedrooms, a sitting-room and kitchen, and an old-fashioned wash-house, that could, later on, be converted quite easily into a bathroom.

Ruth hurried from one room to another, formulating plans. The chocolate brown paintwork, and faded Victorian wallpaper could soon be replaced by cream washed walls and white paintwork. She visualised plain dark carpets on the floors, and warm velvet curtains at the windows. Bits of brass and bright copper, and a few strategically-placed mirrors. Furniture, especially chosen to fit into the small, low rooms, could be bought in gradually, piece by piece.

She spent that week-end making lists of the things she would take to the cottage, and then, on reflection, struck out every item. So much of the contents of The Mullions, she now realised, had been chosen by Harry. She was shocked to discover that over the years he had managed to leave his indelible mark on each room.

But where was she, when Harry had imposed his own style of gracious living on the rooms in her father's house; and how many other facets of her husband had passed her by, unnoticed? Perhaps she had never, after all, really known Harry Flemming?

There had been no precise moment in which she discovered

that she had been cheated by Harry; no instant of dramatic revelation. It had been a permeation of disillusion; an absorption of knowledge through the pores.

He had never been an actor by profession: but he was, by instinct, a natural performer. Harry had the actor's fine and ringing presence. People frequently made flattering assumptions about him. Judgements, which, in the end would turn out to be completely unfounded. The masks he wore, were the only indication Ruth ever had of the man behind them; and they were put on, or altered, to suit every separate occasion.

Oh, Harry Flemming had been careful! Deceptively, hypocritically careful. How he had smiled as he lied about his movements. How shocked he had professed to be, when acquaintances carried on extra-marital affairs, without ever being caught out by their unsuspecting wives! But he was, after all, she supposed only protecting his own investment.

4.

There is nothing quite so inhibiting as an old guilt. Which seemed to explain the constriction in Ruth's throat when she found Georgina and her car in The Mullions driveway on that Monday evening. It had been some years since Georgina's last visit. Her sister, in a suit of delicate blue angora and an Italian perfume, both looked and smelled expensive. As they embraced, a strand of the long flaxen hair fell forward and clung to Ruth's shoulder. She looped it back gently behind Georgina's ear; smoothing it flat with careful fingers; persuading herself that this was still her little sister.

'You look tired Gina. Why didn't you 'phone ahead and tell me you were coming. I would have arranged to be here.'

'Spur of the moment decision, darling! We finished filming this morning, and I suddenly had this irresistible urge to come up and see you.'

'Nothing wrong, is there?'

'Of course not. I'm just a bit weary: I need a few days in your calming presence.'

Georgina hesitated on the step of the storm-porch, almost as if she was unwilling to enter the house. Ruth saw her sister's eyes flicker over the space on the wall where the Lowry had hung and the dent in the dark blue carpet; and she braced herself for the inevitable question. But none was forthcoming.

Ruth made buttered toast and coddled eggs, and mugs of hot, milky cocoa; their childhood panacea for broken dolls and promises. She could see the speedwell-eyes taking in the sticky rings on the kitchen units, and the dust and disorder that was the measure of Ruth's present discontent.

'Ruthie – what's wrong here?'

'Oh – I'm moving out at the week-end.' She began at the end of the story, which seemed as sensible a place as any other, in the circumstances. 'Harry and I are no longer living together: and I've had the offer of this wonderful little old cottage –'

'Where is he, Ruth? Where's Harry?' The question was posed with such urgency that Ruth could not, at once, answer.

'I – well, I don't really know, Gina. He told Clive Jessop at the factory that he was off to New York on a selling mission. But he took the poacher and the egg-timing gadget. I thought that he might have gone into the country.'

'Harry? Ruth – you know how he loves his little comforts. He'd never have gone into the country. He loathes it. Especially in January.'

They gazed at one another for a moment, and then Georgina said, 'So what's happening about the factory?'

Ruth bit her lower lip. 'The Receiver has been called in. We're bankrupt.'

'And Harry Flemming's done a bunk and left you!'

'Well, yes. That seems to sum it up pretty neatly.' She waited for her sister's quite predictable next question, concerning The Mullions and its contents; but once again, the expected question was not forthcoming.

Ruth said, 'I feel badly about you, Gina. I always have

52

done. I wanted to settle some shares in the business on you: and now it's too late. I know it was planned that you should inherit Mother's money, but still –'

'I want nothing, Ruthie. You know very well that Father didn't like me. He always disapproved of the rackety life I lead. He knew what he was doing; I would have blued all his money in less than a year.'

'I don't seem to have done so much better.'

'Not your fault, darling. Blame that little rat Harry for what's happened.' Georgina's voice grew intense. 'You must find him, darling. Let me help you!'

'Oh, be sensible Gina. Where would we start looking; and to what purpose? Let him go!'

'He was never right for you, Ruthie.'

'I know that, now. I suppose I got married for all the wrong reasons.'

'Do you mind all that much? I mean – did you really care very much for him?'

Ruth sighed. 'It was time for me to take a good long look at my life, Gina. See things as they really are – and not as I would have them be. I've always played games, you know. I pretended that if I only made the effort I might even be rather attractive. I tried to convince myself that Harry really loved me, in his way. I deluded myself, didn't I? But,' she waved a hand at her surroundings, 'it's so easy to do that, in a house like this.'

Georgina laughed uncertainly, and got up from her chair to look out the window. 'You know something Ruth? You've become quite a dangerous person ever since you took up this counselling job among the deprived. Why – even I, sometimes find that I have a ridiculous urge to blab all my secrets to you.'

Ruth smiled. 'The service is entirely free, and completely confidential, madam.'

They gazed in the general direction of one another; but their eyes did not meet.

Ruth asked for, and was granted, two week leave of absence from the Mainstay office. Imogen Hirst asked no questions. 'I'm pleased that you're moving down here, among us, Ruth. It's a nice little cottage. I think you'll be comfortable in it.'

She placed a hand on Ruth's forearm. 'Just let us know if we can help in any way, won't you?'

Georgina, meanwhile, seemed unnaturally ill at ease in The Mullions. She wandered from room to room, opening drawers and cupboards, and idly rifling through their contents. Her promise of help with the sorting and packing seemed to be forgotten. Ruth was finding her sister unusually tense and inquisitorial. She continued to ask about Harry.

'Where can he be, Ruth?'

'I don't know.'

'But darling, you must have some kind of suspicion. Nobody just vanishes like that in a puff of green smoke.'

'If I knew I would tell you, Gina.'

'Oh, how can you be so controlled!' she burst out. 'Don't you ever want to let rip and throw things?'

Ruth put down the plate she was wrapping. 'Look,' she said quietly, 'if I rant and scream it won't make any difference. Harry's gone – end of story. He didn't intend that I should ever find him. He actually went to great lengths to prevent it.'

Georgina sighed. 'What a mess it all is.'

'I thought so myself,' said Ruth, 'until I discovered the Friar's Walk cottage.'

Georgina had started to fidget again among the packing-cases; nervously moving all Ruth's carefully sorted books and papers, and putting them down again somewhere else in a different order. 'About this cottage, Ruth. It does sound pretty basic; not really your style at all. In fact, this whole business – this job of yours – the "good deeds in a naughty world" bit –'

'What about it?'

'I worry about you, Ruthie. Are you quite sure you know what you're doing. Why don't we sit down and talk it all over?'

'There's nothing to discuss. Voluntary work is what I do.'

'I know: I know: and it's all very worthy of you, darling. But it does sound such a drag; and surely that's a very rough district you're going into?'

Ruth's voice sank dangerously low. 'And what would you know about that Georgina? After all, it was your idea that I should do the damned job in the first place.'

'We-ell, I once knew a film-crew who worked on a documentary about the St Joseph's district. They told me about it.'

'Gina – I already spend two-thirds of my life in that part of the city. Living down there isn't going to make all that much difference.' Ruth attempted a smile. 'Remember what you once told me: police woman, hospital matron, prison wardress?'

Georgina looked embarrassed. 'Oh hell,' she said, 'look, I'm sorry I ever said that. It was just one of those stupid, slick remarks that I once used to think were so bloody clever.'

Ruth's sister in thoughtful mood was rare enough, but Georgina contrite and apologetic was more than she could bear. 'Things aren't really as bad as they look. I still have my annuity from Grandmother.'

'He's ruined your life, Ruth.'

'Only if I let him.'

'You once wanted children.'

Ruth winced, and turned away to the cupboard that held drinks and glasses. Gin, according to Paisley Smith, was good medicine for most ills. A half-bottle later Georgina said, 'I'm going back to London tomorrow.'

## 5.

Dropping into the Bird in Hand bar like this, could, she thought, quite easily become habitual. Since her first visit with Sam Bright, Ruth surprised herself at times, by visiting the pub unaccompanied in her lunch hour.

She liked to sit in a corner, by the window, and alternately study the life in the bar, and the square outside. She no longer sipped dry martinis but, as the spring days grew warmer, she drank cider from a thick glass tankard.

Viewed from this side of the square, from the Bird in Hand

55

window, Number Seven Friar's Walk looked squat and threatened. Memory was unkind, and no matter how persuasively she might straighten or bend it, the past, like a damaged muscle, would no longer spring back at her command.

Crouched as it was, between two taller houses of greater distinction, the cottage reminded her of herself: trapped as she had always been, between her mother and Georgina.

The heavy brass key in her handbag was opening many doors. On her way through the square that morning, she had noticed the buds on the sycamore trees, and the aching green of the grass. The churchyard was ringed with slate and granite headstones, Canon Flint, that neat and tidy cleric, had recently ordered, that to facilitate the cutting of the grass, all gravestones should be lifted, and moved to lean up against the low perimeter walls. They stood now, like the pages of an ancient book, propped open to tell a long-forgotten story. Ruth paused on her way to the cottage, to decipher some lettering that had been blurred by time and weather.

HERE LIETH MARY CROFTON. WIFE OF SAMUEL.
AND HER DEAR CHILDREN. ELIZA. HENRY.
GEORGE AND ANN.
WHO ALL PERISHED OF THE FEVER.
IN THE YEAR OF OUR LORD. 1757.

Poor Samuel! Did he ever recover from his loss? Or did he wrap himself in mourning, until his own name was added to the roll-call, ten years later?

Ruth moved out of The Mullions two days later. The decision as to what she should take with her, or leave behind, was much easier than she had expected. The cottage, without any consultation, spoke up for itself and rejected Harry's elegant walnut and rosewood, his pale Chinese carpets, and tinkling chandeliers. The furniture van transported no more than the bed, with its linked wicker-hearts, a low armchair upholstered in dark red velvet; the blue-ringed storage jars and copper saucepans; and the trunks that contained her clothing and linen. She had unloaded all responsibility for what remained in The Mullions onto her unwilling solicitor, who would, no doubt make her pay dearly for so doing.

The removal men showed concern. Her transition from the opulence of The Mullions down to Friar's Walk seemed to strike them as highly improbable; they crowded around her in the dark little hallway, unwilling to depart without some reassurance.

'But I intend to furnish gradually,' she insisted. 'It will be so much easier for me to re-decorate if the floors are bare and the house almost empty.'

As she closed the front door behind them Ruth could hear the dark beams creak and settle above her head. This was a house full of sounds and secrets. If she banged a door, loose plaster would rattle softly somewhere overhead.

Perhaps that same Mary Crofton, wife of Samuel, had once lived here. Perhaps she was still up there, in the unused attic-rooms, watching over her four sick infants. Perhaps they could see Ruth Flemming now: those poor, sad spirits whose bones lay so close, by the churchyard wall.

Because unfamiliar surroundings had made her loneliness tangible, she whispered, experimentally; 'Mary? Mary Crofton? Can you hear me? Did you live here once, long ago, when the house was a new one? Did you come as a bride, with your Samuel?'

She sat down on the shallow stone step that led up to the kitchen. Feeling foolish, but compelled to continue, she said in a stronger voice, 'I'll make a pact with you, Mary. Don't leave me! Stay around here, and see how I'll transform your cottage.'

She began to unpack, transferring china and saucepans into built-in kitchen cupboards that reached from floor to ceiling. Left with two empty tea-chests she upended and pushed them together, creating for herself an instant kitchen table. This unsuspected streak of ingenuity restored her self-confidence, and she filled the kettle, plugged it in, and began to hunt for the coffee.

The tall jar of 'instant' was not where she had put it. She worried about this curious lapse, until she remembered Georgina, frantically packing and repacking, on that last evening. Ten minutes later the coffee turned up, unexpectedly, underneath a neatly-packed pile of sheets and blankets.

Ruth's anxiety over the missing coffee – exaggerated, far beyond what was normal – linked her up to her sister once again in a way she was not yet ready to deal with. She remembered the pacing and prowling; all that agitated searching! All those questions about Harry.

'Harry in the country?' Gina had said. 'Ruth – you know how he loves his little comforts. He'd never have gone to live in the country. Especially in January.'

But no one had ever told Georgina the exact date of Harry's defection. She and Harry had always professed to loathe one another. Gina spoke of Harry as 'that self-important tailor's dummy'. Harry had dismissed Georgina as being 'an empty-headed clothes-horse'.

She sat on the edge of the bed, coffee mug in hand, until darkness crept into the square, blurring church tower and gravestones; so that St Joseph's church became a faint charcoal image of itself. Because she was tired and alone in the strange little house, Ruth felt frightened. She resisted the temptation to cross over the road and seek out Sam Bright in the warmth of the Bird in Hand bar.

She had, she now realised, forgotten to bring curtains for this room in which, for the present at least, she would be obliged to eat, sleep and live. She rooted around in the trunk that held linen, and came up with a green cotton tablecloth, that would, with the aid of a few strategically placed thumb tacks, make an adequate temporary cover; and was it only last week that Ruth Flemming had upbraided poor Della Smith for fastening her curtains to the Nelson Street windows with a half-dozen six-inch nails?

She opened her eyes the next morning, and forgetting the tablecloth at the window, wondered vaguely why the daylight should be green-tinted. She took in the room; the walls splashed with cabbage roses: and the chipped brown paintwork that had seen Mrs Pomeroy out through the reigns of several monarchs.

She could hear the emptiness. That beautiful, soothing, hollow sound of rooms that hold nothing but air and ancient dust. How heavily the family possessions must have weighed upon her! In this shabby cottage, in these small bare rooms, why – she could be mistaken for almost anybody. Already her standards were slipping. Last night, she had pinned a tablecloth over her window, and ate doorstep jam-sandwiches from an up-ended packing-case table.

There were ten rooms in The Mullions. In that rarefied air, mahogany elbowed walnut, silver outshone crystal, velvet competed with brocade to catch the eye. Possessions. Things to be looked at, but not handled. To be proud of, but not loved.

On this first morning in Friar's Walk Ruth bathed with spectacular difficulty, since she was a very tall woman, in a small plastic bowl, in the only few inches of water she had been able to heat up in the electric kettle.

This, she now realised, must be normal, everyday procedure among people who had no bathroom.

6.

The appearance of a dark blue car in St Joseph's Square on a Saturday morning, caused several people to experience a fluttering sensation in the region of chest and breastbone. As it edged away into Friar's Walk, craned heads were lowered from the windows of Dino's café; and pint pots were offered up for a hasty refill in the Bird in Hand bar. The realisation that it was not yet their turn with Detective Sergeant McInnes was sufficient to pitch the laughter a little louder, and raise a sweat of relief between shoulder blades that had, just for a second or two, felt exposed.

The shabby charm of the square on an April morning could hardly be expected to reach a man like McInnes. He was only conscious of the plotting skinheads in Dino's café, of the pimps and thieves who propped up the bar of the Bird in Hand, and of little Billy Evans, who at sight of the patrol car, had slipped smartly away down the alley that gave onto Nelson Street.

As for Ruth, still in dressing-gown and slippers, and carefully unpinning the improvised curtain from her front window, the appearance of McInnes at her door was no more than an untimely intrusion.

'Mrs Flemming. They told me at Mainstay that I'd find you here.' He waited, 'Aren't you going to ask me in then? I need to ask you a few question.' The voice and the manner were stiff with assumptions. The inference being, of course, that he was strong and she was weak. That he was wise and she was foolish. That he was a seeker after truth, and she, because of her connection with Mainstay, would be bound to conceal something from him. He was also angry.

Ruth could sense the rawness in him. It seeped through his policeman's grudging façade of official politeness, adding an extra edge to his tone and his gestures. She stepped back to allow him to enter, and tried not to smile as he cracked his head on a beam. They moved into the little front room, and McInnes at once looked about for a place to sit down. The red velvet chair was clearly too low to accommodate his exceptional height, and since Ruth had already claimed the bed, he could hardly, in view of his official dignity, join her there; visibly put out, he was forced to stand.

'We received a report that some squatters had moved in here.' The words, innocuous in themselves, and delivered in a strong Geordie accent, were, nevertheless, flung out at Ruth like a challenge.

'But surely,' she said quietly, 'they told you at Mainstay that I was now living in this cottage?'

'Oh yes. But I didn't believe them. I know where you live – madam. I was up in that area last summer on enquiries. I saw you then, working in your garden.'

'Well, as you can see, Sergeant McInnes, I no longer live in Hillcrest. I am not a squatter, neither am I holding this front door open for others to come in and squat. Check with Canon Flint if you don't believe me! He'll confirm that I'm in legal possession here. I have a key and a rent book.'

The policeman's long bony face showed nothing; he gained time by adjusting the set of his smart grey jacket and settling the gold-rimmed spectacles more firmly upon his nose. 'Hmn,' he said, accusingly, 'you're a bit short on furniture aren't you for a permanent tenant?'

Wearily, Ruth explained once again that in view of her plans for redecoration it seemed wiser to leave the cottage unfurnished, for the present. She pointed out the bed and the chair. 'As you can see, I'm managing in one room, at the moment.'

McInnes stared at the bare brown room, the uncurtained window, and the small sad huddle of her few possessions. 'You must be finding it a bit of a come down after living in Hillcrest.' And then, casually, 'Mr Flemming living here with you, is he?'

Ruth hesitated. To lie would be pointless, yet she was strangely reluctant to volunteer this man any more information. 'I'm alone at present,' she said lamely.

He grinned. 'Hubby been a bit naughty, has he? Well, it happens.' He pointed at the window. 'Just you watch your step, that's all. This is a violent "manor". Not at all a suitable neighbourhood for a well brought-up lady like yourself.'

The condescension in his tone made her reckless. 'Perhaps you've never noticed,' Ruth said sharply, 'that in all the years I've worked here, not one of your "violent" people has ever laid a hand on me. I walk where I choose, unhampered. I don't offer provocation.' She smiled, sweetly. 'How good is your own record in that respect, Sergeant?'

McInnes fingered the old, livid scar on his forehead, and a redness crept out from beneath his clean white collar. 'Don't try to be too bloody clever,' he advised her, 'we've got the lot down in this division. The muggers and rapists. The cranks and the borderline nutters.' He grinned, wolfishly. 'I've watched you, Mrs Flemming. Seen you come in the mornings and drive home in the evenings. Commuting I expect you call it. And what is it you do here? A few easy hours of your so-called counselling each day? Hand out a few chittys for hot soup and blankets? Then revert back to type, up in Hillcrest.'

'That annoys you, Sergeant?'

'Lady, I'll tell you something. People like you get right up my nose!'

A strand of grey hair fell across his forehead, and he thrust it away with an irritable gesture. For some reason. Ruth found herself vaguely reminded of Harry.

'Is that why you really came here this morning,' she asked him, 'to warn me?'

This time he grinned with genuine amusement. 'I wanted to see how the other half lives. Well, now I know, don't I?'

The big blue car pulled away from Friar's Walk, and the skinheads in Dino's window raised their coffee mugs in salute as it passed. Mrs Mandelbaum watched, broad and dark, in her narrow doorway; and Sam Bright, who had one foot across the Bird in Hand threshold, looked more worried than usual as Detective Sergeant McInnes drove by.

He should not have able to upset her. The fact that he had done so, and without even trying, alarmed her. She went into the kitchen and brewed up a large pot of coffee, and then drank it too quickly so that it scalded her lips and her throat.

Perhaps this Sergeant McInnes had come to assess her? She had seen how the questions had flickered and held in those bleak grey eyes. 'Rich bitch?' he had asked himself; or a bored female on the look-out for some cheap excitement? Perhaps he saw her as some sort of religious nut who had hitched her wagon to the star of Mainstay? He had hinted that the streets of St Joseph's were crawling with people who nursed strange obsessions.

Detective Sergeant McInnes. A hard man, so they said. One who seemed to enjoy being hated. People told him things; men like Billy Evans. Little, obliging, cringing men who would always need favours. Sam Bright had once warned her about him. 'Man's a bastard, Ruth. He detests the whole bloody world, and everybody in it. Decent coppers cross the street when they see McInnes coming.'

Ruth began to make her bed, dragging at the sheets and shaking up the duvet with unnecessary force. Disturbed, in a way she had never been before the policeman's visit, she pulled on her old blue raincoat, snatched up her purse, and went out to buy paint.

The man in the paintshop was reassuringly helpful. Having once recognised her ignorance of his subject, he grew lyrical. 'Magnolia,' he enthused, investing that word with a tender magic. 'Magnolia emulsion is what you want, madam. Cover anything, that will!'

They discussed the state of her walls. 'Dry,' she confirmed, 'with the wallpaper firmly attached since Victoria's reign. No – not really dirty. More like dull and gloomy.'

He sold her a selection of brushes, and a brown plastic tray with a lambswool roller resting in it. 'Give it three or four coats,' he instructed, 'if you want a good finish.' She began with the bedroom: the one at the front of the house, with the sloping stone floor and the two long windows. Her technique with the roller and tray, although shaky at first, improved as she worked. She pushed up the two sash windows and let in the warm spring air; and as one coat of magnolia emulsion dried out, she applied another. Miraculously, the old busy patterns of flower and fern were subsiding. Ruth sat on the floor among brushes and paint-cans, and observed that the walls of the room had truly changed colour. 'As it was, Mary Crofton,' she whispered, 'as it was in the beginning. Cool and clean, and simple.'

The word got around in St Joseph's, and Ruth had her callers. Interested spectators who dropped in to offer her instruction on rubbing down the paintwork, and how to restore old oak beams. Paisley Smith, on her way home from school through St Joseph's churchyard, dragged long ragged grooves in the Canon's gravel with the toes of her worn-out sandals. When she reached Ruth's window she stopped and stared in.

'Is that you, miss?'

'I believe so, Paisley.'

'You look ever-sa mucky. What you doin'?'

The sunshine had brought up a fresh crop of freckles and sharpened the tint of the thick ginger braid on the gypsy child's shoulder. The hem of her torn cotton dress hung down, and she was minus one sock.

Ruth looked at the state of her own dirty clothing and magnolia stained fingers. 'I'm trying to clean this old house up.'

'Can I help you?' the child asked.

Paisley stalked through the rooms like a foreman painter, checking walls and doors. When she came to the bedroom she frowned. 'It's all a bit – a bit plain-like, 'ant it?'

'But that's how I want it, Paisley.'

Ruth's caller dropped down, cross-legged to the dusty stone floor; she looked dreamy.

'Billy's gonna paper my bedroom,' she boasted. 'I already picked out the wallpaper. It's got big pink roses on it.' She sketched the size of the promised blooms in the air. 'An' I'm having a nice pink carpet, an' one of them fancy stools wi' a silk fringe round it. An' a big white wardrobe wi' a mirror an' gold handles.'

Ruth looked down at the top of the small, fiery head and her heart turned over. The pink and white room had to be an impossible dream, vowed by Billy Evans. The child was describing in fine detail, the expensive furniture display that was presently to be seen in a shop in Crimea Street.

'Do you like Billy Evans?'

'He's OK. For a fella.'

Paisley suddenly rushed down the stairs, and out into the wash-house. 'What you goin' to do here, then?'

'Make a bathroom.'

'We 'ant got one 'a them in our house.'

'How do you manage – about washing, I mean?'

'Oh,' Paisley was dismissive on the subject, 'I gets clean when I go swimming. Wi' the school – you know!' She hesitated, ''Cept I got no towel.'

'No towel?'

'I take a bit of old curtain to dry myself on; or an old woolly jumper. The other kids laugh, but I don' care.'

Ruth threw back the lid of the trunk and pulled out a large yellow bathsheet. 'Bring it back,' she warned, 'each time you use it, and I'll wash it for you.'

The child tucked the towel underneath her arm. 'What you havin' for your tea, miss?'

'I don't know. I seem to be living on bread and jam just lately.'

Ruth regarded her thoughtfully. 'Are you hungry, Paisley?'

'Always!'

'What time does the chip shop open?'

'Five o'clock. On the dot.'

Ruth gave her some money. 'You'd better go home first, and tell your mother that you'll be having your supper at my house.'

Paisley grinned. ''Ant no good me goin' home miss. Door's always locked about this time. Ma'll have a boy-friend roun' there. Visitin'-time, tha's what she calls it.'

Ruth sat on the edge of the bed with the packing-case table

wedged firmly between them. Paisley fitted the red chair exactly. She sat primly, all her limbs gathered decorously together. Her feet, in the scuffed brown sandals, tucked carefully out of sight, underneath her chair. She had the strained air of a child who had been forced to attend a formal dinner given by adults. To ease the tension a little, Ruth said, 'These chips are good, aren't they?'

Paisley nodded. 'Don' you ever buy chips from that place in Slade Street. He's real stingy!' Her voice had the rapt intensity of the true gourmet. 'His batter's all soggy in the middle, an' he burns his fish. I always go to old Stavros in the market. I know it's a bit further to walk, but he makes good chips, an' his fish are bigger.'

Paisley cautioned Ruth against chip-shop vinegar. It was bound to be watered-down; she had seen them do it. Tomato sauce, she hinted, was the correct accompaniment to the dish – that was, of course, if you had such a thing in your cupboard?

Ruth felt acutely embarrassed; a hostess caught out by a discerning guest – and at her first house-warming party!

'Never mind, miss. We can get some when you go shopping. Tesco's is best. They got giant-size bottles. Best to get big ones: they last all the longer.'

For the first time in months, Ruth found she could smile with a genuine pleasure. She gazed at the child, and could see that the brief conversation had already relaxed her. Paisley Smith now abandoned the unfamiliar knife and fork, and began to eat quickly, with her fingers; only pausing to wipe off an excess of grease down the front of her dress. She glanced scornfully round her.

'My ma said you was well-off.'

'Did she really?'

Curiosity, and a new mood of fellow-feeling made the child's gruff voice tender. 'Was you chucked-out a' somewhere then, miss?'

'Well, yes,' Ruth said slowly. 'I suppose, in a way, you could say that's exactly what happened.'

Paisley Smith selected a long fat chip; she studied it briefly, and then transferred it luxuriously into her mouth. She chewed for a moment and then swallowed. Reflectively, she said, 'Your ole man got another woman – I betcha'. Don' you worry about it, miss. My ma' says all men is bastards.' She leaned back in the red velvet chair and regarded her empty plate with regret.

'You'll be better-off wi' out him,' she counselled. 'I 'ant never gonna get married.'

Ruth thought she would like to replace the ragged cotton dress with new, soft toned outfits. She would want to dress this child in shades of almond and copper. Green was her colour.

Paisley Smith was not yet too old for dolls; a bicycle for Christmas; a pony for her birthday. Ruth Flemming dreamed about buying party outfits; riding breeches; of ensuring this child clean underwear, and hair she need not continually scratch at.

Regretfully, she said, 'You'd better be off now, Paisley. Your mother will be getting worried.'

Paisley shook her head. 'She don' never worry about me, miss. It's me that worries about her.'

Two weeks of unaccustomed physical effort had left Ruth exhausted. But now all her walls were magnolia coloured, and the chocolate brown paintwork had vanished beneath several coats of brilliant white paint. She had achieved the effect she sought. A clean simple background, against which she might hang her new freedom.

Plain dark carpets had been fitted to cover the cracked and sloping floors; and she walked from room to room on that warm May evening, pausing at strategic corners; imagining a picture here – a gilt mirror there.

The clang of a heavy iron gate drew her back to the window. She could just make out Sergeant McInnes, in the twilight, crossing the churchyard grass on those long, stick-like legs. A dog walked beside him: a thin grey lurcher. The man, unaware that he was being observed, had allowed his shoulders to slump, and his head hang down. The policeman, Ruth thought, looked unhappy.

*Part Three*

# SUMMER

# 1.

The sun returned to the city. Colour washed over St Joseph's until the soft saffron tint of early morning gave way to a deep, dark blue.

In the market they were selling strawberries in green punnets; crisp fresh lettuce, and the first outdoor roses. Already, the pavements felt gritty and hot underfoot.

Summer in the city brought its own brand of madness. Strange obsessions surfaced, and would not be quelled. People lost control. Della Smith grew restless for lane and hedgerow, and muttered madly that she must soon be moving on.

Paisley tossed her broken sandals onto a heap of rotting debris, and was observed running through the churchyard, barefoot. Billy Evans took to wearing a pair of high-heeled scarlet cowboy boots and a cream sombrero he had bought in the second-hand market.

Several local men exposed themselves, and were promptly arrested.

Ruth discovered that on Sunday evenings at six, old ladies in ruched-velvet hats and best coats, carrying prayer-books, came regularly to worship in the great dark church. On Wednesday evenings the practising bell-ringers at the end of a long, hot stint in the belfry, fell across the Bird in Hand doorstep, gasping out their last orders.

There was a brass tray, round and gleaming, in the dark recesses of the Mandelbaums' dusty window. Mrs Mandelbaum, ever watchful, waddled forwards. 'You off visiting then, dearie?'

Ruth smiled. 'Yes I am: and I won't have that long drive down from Hillcrest anymore. I'll have time to look into your shop window in the mornings.'

The dark head, with its complicated arrangements of braids and jet combs, nodded gloomily. 'Well I must say, you got your job sitting right on your front doorstep. Just don't let them take advantage of you, is all!' She gazed malevolently around her at a queue of imaginary clients. 'They will you know, dearie, if you let them.'

The air in the interview room was warm and stale. She hurried to throw up the window, and water the cheese plant, which, neglected for almost two weeks, was beginning to droop in its corner. The Mainstay grapevine, nurtured no doubt, by Sam Bright's intuitive guesses, had obviously received word of her husband's defection.

'How are you managing?' asked Imogen Hirst. 'Are you coping all right on your own?'

Ruth shrugged. 'It wasn't a close kind of marriage. I don't really miss him. It's a relief in a way to have the whole tangle resolved.'

The Organiser looked doubtful. 'You've lost weight Ruth.'

Ruth smiled, 'Two weeks of scrubbing and painting the cottage will account for that.'

The lines in Imogen's face grew deeper. 'I'm sorry to bring you bad news on top of all your other troubles.' She paused, and looked down at the file in her hand. 'Mrs Edith Hardy, Tulip Fields. One of yours, I believe?'

'Why, yes. I call once a fortnight.'

'She's dead, Ruth. An overdose of barbiturates. By the time Jack Hardy had sobered up and realised that she wasn't play-acting, it was all too late.' A note that was faintly accusatory made Ruth stiffen. 'When you last spoke of this lady to us, there was no hint that she might have been suicidal.'

'She wasn't,' Ruth said firmly. 'or at least, I thought that she wasn't.'

Mrs Hardy. She had not asked for too much. A child, at the very beginning; but later on in her marriage she had been prepared to settle for a brand-new house on a city estate. Ruth beat her clenched fist on the desk until the bud-vase moved and the wire tray rattled.

The file was a thick one. It went back a long way, and involved many people. All of them dedicated, on paper, to the salvation of Mrs Hardy.

*City General Hospital. Casualty Dept. February 1st, 1972.*
Broken collar bone. Fractured tibia. Contusions to left side of face. Patient insists that these injuries sustained in fall in her kitchen?
*May 4th, 1972.*
Two fingers broken left hand. Patient reports having trapped her hand in door.
*September 20th, 1972.*
Patient admitted. Severely concussed. Reported by husband as having struck head on doorstep when re-entering house after fetching in washing. Is this patient accident-prone? Or victim of repeated battering?

1972 had been a bad year for Mrs Hardy.

1973 had been marginally better. She had sustained no serious injury in that time. It was about then, that the psychiatrist took her over.
*Mrs Hardy. Edith. White. Married. Childless.*
Person domiciled with patient. *Husband. Jack Ernest Hardy.*
Husband is unable to offer any explanation for his wife's depression. Reports that she is obsessed with cleanliness. (Washing rituals, etc)
Patient has lost weight recently. Experiences difficulties when obliged to leave the house.

There followed an account of the drugs prescribed, and the counselling given. Nothing more was reported about her until late in 1979, when the name of Edith Hardy first appeared in the records of Mainstay.

Helping other people can give an unwarranted sense of power. Especially when first sampled. Mrs Hardy was Ruth's first unqualified success; a woman who broke down and revealed some completely new information; a knowledge of her condition not formerly vouchsafed to hospital staff, or the patient's own doctor.

The breakthrough had come in Ruth's fourth meeting with her. Mrs Hardy, still puffy about lips and eyebrows, seemed less punch-drunk on that occasion. More aware of the dangers inherent in her situation. She had begun with her usual denial that she might need help.

'I didn't want you to come visiting here today. In fact, if you want the truth, I nearly sent a note round to stop you.'

'Why Mrs Hardy?'

'Well, I don't need help. Not from your sort. It's that Dr Fowler. He blackmailed me into letting you come here. What he really wants is for me to go back to the – well, you know – the mental clinic. But I said no. No; I'm all right, really.' She'd glared at Ruth as she said this. 'I just get a bit – well, you know – nervous like, sometimes. It's my age I expect. Mother was the same.'

'How was that?'

'She had nerve trouble. Couldn't eat. Never went out much, neither. Proper home-body my mother was. I'm getting just the same.'

'It's not always such a good idea, Mrs Hardy, to spend too much time in the house. Dr Fowler tells me that you wear yourself out with housework.'

'I like things kept nice. Clean and tidy. Well, you do, don't you?' She'd fixed her eyes on the faded brown wallpaper. 'It's this house that's the trouble. It's old. Old and mucky. No matter what you do, it makes no difference. It's got damp, you see. It smells funny. Like there's something awful rotting away somewhere.' She glanced back at Ruth, and then swiftly away. 'I know it can't be her. I stood by the grave and saw her buried. But it sort of gets on my mind – and then –'

'And then what, Mrs Hardy?'

'I get a bit stroppy. I get on at Jack. Let's sell up, I say. Let's move out to Martree. I'd be better in a nice new house. Away from St Joseph's.'

'And your husband is still unwilling to move?'

'He was born in this house. It belonged to his mother. She lived with us from the day we got married.' Mrs Hardy's gaze had come back and locked onto Ruth. 'I still see her you know Mrs Flemming. She's still there, in that chair in the corner. She watches me.'

'Watches you?'

'She's been dead seven years; but she never "went", if you know what I mean.'

'Yes,' Ruth said slowly, 'I do know what you mean.'

'She spoilt Jack rotten. He was her only one. She give him everything he asked for. Thought I should do the same.'

'And did you?'

'I did at first. Well, you do, don't you. Spoil them a bit I mean, when you're first married. Jack was a good-looking chap in them days. Before the drink got him.'

'Was he always a heavy drinker?'

'They used to go out together. Round the Bird in Hand every night of the week. She liked her pint, same as Jack did.'

'You never went with them?'

'I can't stand noise, Mrs Flemming; and the smoke in that pub made my eyes run. Besides: they never wanted me to go with them. They had each other.'

'I see.'

Mrs Hardy had grown tense. She clasped her hands tightly together. 'He never got over it, you know. Her dying and leaving him behind. Not that she did – not really. Like I tell him, the evil old bitch is still with us, watching everything we do. Spying on us.'

'What happens when you say that to him?'

'That's when he – hits me.'

'Does that happen very often?'

'It's my own fault. I know if I keep going on about his mother, it'll happen. But I can't seem to help it somehow. I – I reckon I goad him.'

'How do you goad him?'

'Mother's boy, I call him. Can't sell the furniture because she bought it. Always paints the house the same colour because she chose it. Nobody has chocolate and cream anymore, do they? I wanted a nice bright yellow front door. Something cheerful. He even plants the same flowers in the garden as she did. Can't ever sell the house, he says; Mother wouldn't like it. We got no children. Did you know that?'

'Yes, you mentioned –'

'Not my fault! Him – he don't want any children. Like I told him – bloody great kid yourself, that's what you are! No room for a baby in this house, is there? Not with you in it.'

'What happened that time?'

'That's when he – well – that's when I got the concussion.'

'Was it bad?'

'I was knocked out for hours. Oh, it scared him. Don't tell anybody, he said, don't say that I did it. I'll make it up to you when you come home.'

'And did he?'

Mrs Hardy laughed, briefly. 'He took me to Blackpool for the weekend. To see the illuminations. That's when he brought me the first horse-and-wagon.'

'Horse-and-wagon?'

'I got dozens of 'em Mrs Flemming. Look at 'em, all round the house. Models: made of plastic and china. I saw one in this gift shop on the sea-front. "I like that, Jack," I said to him. So he bought it for me. After that, it become a habit like. Every time he hits me he goes out afterwards and buys me another horse-and-wagon. I got dozens all over the house.'

'You've never mentioned any of this before, Mrs Hardy.'

'It's easier with another woman, Mrs Flemming. You're about my age too.' She paused. 'I can trust you, can't I? They say that you're like the Catholic priest; not allowed to tell what you hear?'

'That's right. I won't reveal anything that you want to tell me.'

'That's OK then.' She'd relaxed slightly, and rubbed her forehead. 'I'd got to such a pitch; you know how it is, don't you? I'd just got to talk to somebody. Sometimes I feel my head'll burst. It's since that concussion, really. Aspirin don't seem to touch it.'

'Perhaps Dr Fowler could give you –'

'Don't you mention doctors to me! They all think I'm loony anyway.'

Ruth had said, tentatively, 'I could have a chat with Mr Hardy, if you think he'd be willing.'

At once, Edith Hardy had come upright in her chair. 'Oh no, for God's sake don't ever do that. Jack 'ud kill me if he found out that I'd been telling you about, well – personal things. No. I tell you what! You let me come round to

Mainstay and have a chat with you.'

'Have you ever thought of calling the police,' Ruth had asked her. 'Sometimes, you know, the very fact that he's been arrested will act as a deterrent on a violent man.'

'Police! Don't make me laugh. They're men aren't they? I once worked with a woman whose husband beat her senseless. She went down the Bridewell and showed them what he'd done. Do you know what Sergeant McInnes told her? Go home, missus. Cook your old man his favourite dinner. Kiss and make-up.'

Mrs Hardy had shaken her head. 'That woman died of a brain haemorrhage ten days later.'

Her fortnightly visits to Mrs Hardy had begun in October 1979. For almost ten months they faced one another across a table. She had talked, Ruth had listened. She was to be Mrs Hardy's salvation. Her Guru. Ruth had thought she seemed less apathetic just lately: more alive.

Mrs Hardy had said, 'They say that you're coming to live down here; in that dark little house beside the church. I don't know how you can do that. Live in St Joseph's from choice, I mean. What does your hubby think about moving?'

'It doesn't concern him, anymore. We no longer live together.'

'Oh. Oh, I see. Won't you feel scared then, living by yourself? It gets a bit rough round here, at the weekend.'

Ruth smiled. 'I think I'll be safe enough.'

Edith Hardy smiled back. 'I'll be moving myself, pretty soon,' she had said, 'to a nice new place.'

'Really? Has your husband agreed then –?'

'Well – no.' She'd looked puzzled but happy. 'I was told it see. By a fortune-teller. It's all there in my hand, so she said. A bright new building. Lovely garden; full of flowers. She could see it: plain as daylight.'

'Who told you all this, Mrs Hardy, was it Della Smith the gypsy?'

Ruth's client had looked defensive. 'She tells true. Everybody says so. You can always tell when a gypsy gets onto the truth. They look sort of scared-like, don't they?'

Everything about the crematorium was bright and new.

Lovely garden; full of flowers. Concrete, plate-glass, blonde wood, discrete lighting. Interior design by Habitat. Decor by courtesy of the City Council. Against the advice of her Organiser and colleagues, Ruth attended Mrs Hardy's funeral. Death, she thought, belonged properly to old, dark places. Like St Joseph's churchyard. There was a rushed service, a speedy cremation; and in no time at all the wreaths were set out in the summer heat for the mourners to see and admire.

Jack Hardy was dangerously sober.

As Ruth set her spray of white roses down among all the other tributes, he said, 'Messed her up pretty good between us, didn't we, you and me!'

Ruth turned round to face him. The swollen eyes barely fitted his narrow face, and his hands were shaking.

'What was it you told her, then?' he asked savagely. 'You promised her a brand new house, didn't you? You had no right to do that. It was after I'd told her to forget it; that there was nothing doing, that she –' He turned away, unable to continue.

Later on, in the smoky gloom of the Bird in Hand bar, Ruth asked Sam Bright, 'Would it have made any difference if I had been in the office that Monday?'

'None at all.'

'Perhaps I should have pinned a notice on the door. "In case of emergency please come to seven Friar's Walk."'

Sam was angry. 'Start doing that, and you'll be the next candidate for a nervous breakdown. People die, Ruth. It's part of life. You can't play God. Oh yes, you might have talked her out of it, this time. But there would have been other days and nights.'

# 2.

The plumber was a little brown man called Arthur, who
smoked a pipe. He wore baggy trousers, a scarlet embroidered waistcoat, and no shirt. His arms and chest were
heavily tattooed with designs which she thought it wiser not
to examine too closely. He arrived, surreptitiously, after
dark, in a plain brown van, having been recommended by
Billy Evans as cheap, reliable and speedy.

Arthur took measurements haphazardly, with an odd
length of wood he just happened to find propped up against
her back doorstep. He bit on the stem of his empty briar pipe
and considered the size of the wash-house.

'Not much room in here, is there? I can do you a lav, a
shower and a wash-basin. Nothin' fancy. Plain white. Do
your own tiling and decorating.'

The figure he quoted for achieving this miracle was so low
that she at once accepted it.

Arthur moved into Friar's Walk on a Monday morning. By
Wednesday evening he had departed, cash in hand; leaving
behind him a lav, a shower and a wash-basin, all in working
order. On Thursday Ruth found time to purchase pale-blue
shower curtains, several packs of blue tiles, and a role of blue
carpet.

Paisley Smith found Ruth's style of home-making a strange
and uniquely 'gorgio' phenomenon.

'All blue?' she asked. 'What you want it all blue for?' She
kicked at the roll of carpet and fingered the packs of tiles. 'I'd
a' had yellow, if it was me. Yellow's like sunshine. Like that
towel you give me. I like yellow.'

'Too late now,' Ruth said briskly. 'I should have consulted
you earlier Paisley; but I've bought blue now – so blue it will
have to be.'

Paisley sat cross-legged on the floor and watched as Ruth
scraped at the peeling grey walls of the putative bathroom.
'You shoulda' seen my gran's van,' she boasted, 'it's a lot
nicer'n this old house o'yours.'

'I'm sure it is,' Ruth agreed, although she believed no such thing. 'Tell me about it.'

'Well – she's got real lace curtains, and the windows got flowers scratched on 'em – you know, on the glass.'

'Engraved?'

' 'Spect so. An' she's got cupboards all full o' cup an' plates and stuff. I'm not allowed to touch it. It's called "Crown" something.'

'Crown Derby?'

'That's right. It's lovely inside my gran's van.'

'Do you miss it?'

Paisley chewed on the end of her pigtail. 'My ma can't read and write. Did you know that?'

Ruth nodded.

'She don' even know how to use the phone-box, my ma don't.' She paused. 'Uncle Sol chucked her out. Did you know that?'

'I guessed as much, Paisley.'

'They shouted at her, an' said she brought shame on the family.' Paisley frowned. 'Tha's not fair, miss. She can't work the cooker nor the telly. Billy calls her a "thicko". Never know what the silly bitch'll do next; tha's what Billy says.'

'Look,' said Ruth, 'don't keep calling me "miss". I'm not your schoolteacher. Just call me Ruth.'

The radio mast on the new Police Station soared higher than St Joseph's steeple. The only building of any significance to stand in between them, was the Mainstay office.

On fine summer evenings she observed that Sergeant McInnes came to exercise his grey lurcher dog in the churchyard. Quite probably on wet ones too. Since taking on the task of cleaning out the porches and sweeping the paths, Ruth felt that she had certain 'caretaker' rights in the matter.

The sight of the dog, defecating in among the gravestones annoyed her.

'I don't think you should let her do that, Mr McInnes,' she shouted from the safety of her own front porch.

'Mind your own bloody business,' McInnes shouted back.

'It's against the law,' she cried hopefully.

'Prove it,' growled McInnes.

The little rumpus, like so many of the uncouth exchanges that took place in the square, had begun to embarrass her. She moved across to the low church wall, so that she need not shout quite so loudly. McInnes and his growling dog came towards her.

'That's hallowed ground,' Ruth said primly.

'Hallowed, my arse,' said the policeman, 'it's the only bit of grass for miles around. Everybody comes here.'

'Then shouldn't you be setting an example?'

'Oh my God,' he groaned wearily, 'what the hell has it got to do with you where my dog does its business?'

'I clean the paths and the porches, Sergeant.'

'Come again?'

'The paths and the church porches – I clean them. It's a condition of the tenancy of my cottage.'

McInnes grinned. 'Now I've heard it all! Look Mrs Flemming – tell you what I'll do. I'll bring round a brush and dustpan so that you can crawl round the churchyard sweeping up the dog-turds.'

The hairs on the dog's thin neck began to bristle, and low threatening noises issued from her throat. Passers-by were pausing to stare curiously at the odd little tableau.

'As a matter of fact,' said McInnes, off-handedly, 'I was just on my way round to see you.'

'What is it this time?' Ruth asked him. 'Am I suspected of harbouring escaped convicts?'

Before he could answer, or she could prevent him, McInnes had vaulted the low stone wall, and marched in through her open front door. She followed him into the kitchen with every intention of telling him to leave, but he had already seated himself on her packing-case table.

'I saw Speedy's van outside this house,' he said abruptly.

'Speedy?'

'Red waistcoat. Rude tattoos. Drives a small brown van.'

'Oh – you mean Arthur,' her tone was wary, 'he dropped in for a chat.'

'Arthur?' McInnes snickered, 'you don't mean to tell me that he needs an "agony aunty"?'

She ignored the sarcasm. 'He came round to do some plumbing work for me.'

Belligerently, she threw open the door that led into the bathroom. 'Look – he did all that – singlehanded.'

McInnes stood beside her, and whistled softly. 'Nicked,'

he whispered, 'the whole bloody lot. I'll swear to it. A plumber's warehouse was done a few weeks ago.' Accusingly, he said, 'Who brought him round here – was it Evans?'

'No,' she lied, 'I just happened to hear about him. That he did odd jobs for people in his spare time.'

'He does that all right.' McInnes went back to the upended packing-case, sat down, and took up the study of his toe-caps. 'Didn't happen to leave anything behind, did he? The odd shower tray or wash-basin; in a shed or an outhouse. Ask you to store a few things for him maybe?'

Ruth bridled. 'What sort of fool do you think I am? Why don't you search my house while you're in here. Everything is mine. I have bills to prove it.' She paused, and smiled sweetly at him. 'Perhaps you can advise me, Sergeant? I was planning to buy a few things from the junk shop on the corner. But are they to be trusted? Tell me – is there a chance that the Mandelbaums might be international fences who are using that little business as a cover?'

McInnes considered her coldly for some moments. 'Shall I tell you your trouble?' he said, at last. 'You're an interfering busybody. A so-called do-gooder with too much time on her hands; one of the "ladies in hats" brigade. You're in danger of crossing over to the other side, Mrs Flemming. If you're not very careful you'll come up against the law yourself; and in your position you can't afford to do that.'

'What do you know about my position?'

'If you want the truth, you Mainstay people are a bloody nuisance. Always underfoot; bleating and protesting – withholding information.'

'Do all policemen hold that opinion?'

'I don't speak for the others,' snapped McInnes. 'I march to my own drum.'

The policeman's assured aggression appalled her. As he spoke, all the bones in his face stood out, sharp and ugly. In the same ragged tone he continued, 'I saw you out at the cemetery the other day. I reckon you got a pretty rough ride from Jack Hardy.'

'No more than I'd expected. Mr Hardy will, naturally, want to act the part of the grief-stricken husband; now that it's all too late.'

'What does that mean?'

'Edith Hardy was a battered wife. But you don't have any time for them either, do you Sergeant?' In her most convinced and patronising tone Ruth said, 'Take a look behind any suicidal woman – and you'll be sure to find a guilt-ridden husband lurking somewhere.'

'My wife,' said McInnes quietly, 'my wife, Marion, killed herself last summer.'

## 3.

On Saturday morning Sam Bright called round, and Ruth asked him to help her with moving the bed upstairs. She could, she supposed, have made the same use of Detective Sergeant McInnes, but her relationship with him was not quite of the type that permitted the asking of favours. Surprisingly, since the policeman's last visit, she had been filled with a curious compulsion to put her house in order. Remembering a low, pie-crust table in the Mandelbaums' window, she rushed out to buy it.

'And I'll take the brass tray while I'm here,' she said rashly, not even stopping to enquire the price. Ruth closed her eyes, and imagined the bedroom. The bed, king-sized because it had been chosen by Harry, took up most of the floor-space. All she would need would be a night-table, a lamp or two, and a wardrobe.

Mrs Mandelbaum, scenting business, asked slyly, 'What else you short of then dearie? You got kitchen stuff?'

'No, I haven't.'

'I got nice pine dresser, out back. Matching chairs and table, if you want. Is all good stuff: no schmutter! Maybe wants bit of repairing – I let you have cheap, Mrs Flemming.'

She also bought a fridge and a cooker; and a rug for the kitchen. Once again she would need Billy Evans, and Speedy, whose handy brown van could be used to transport things.

Ruth fitted into Seven Friar's Walk with the ease of an aching foot that had long sought a comfortable slipper. For the past ten years she had lived with her husband's taste, and before that, the fine antiques that had been her grandparents' choice. Now, she was free to choose. Shapes, colours, textures. Friends even? She thought about McInnes. Now there was a man, who, for some obscure reason needed to be hated. He really did, she concluded, go out of his way to antagonise people. Not at all like Harry, who had wriggled and fawned, and crawled through life; licking all the right boots, of all the "best" people.

Loneliness. The word had a toneless quality. It described a state of mind that was solitary, disconnected; something so threatening that she could never, personally, admit to suffering from it. It had always seemed to her that loneliness was a self-imposed torment.

Nobody knew about that one year of madness in which she had attempted to steal other women's babies. Whether or not he was aware of his state of mind, Ruth believed that Detective Sergeant McInnes was a lonely and unhappy man.

Her purchases from the junk and curio shop were delivered on a warm summer's evening by Speedy and Billy Evans. Since the chesterfield was too wide to come in through the tiny front door, they were obliged to remove both sections of the broader sash-window. Once inside, they placed her furniture in position, and then sat down together on the red leather cushions. They bounced experimentally, like children, testing out the springs. Ruth offered them tea or coffee – or something stronger, but Billy glanced nervously out of the window, and then declined. As she watched the small brown van pull away from Friar's Walk and into the square, the reason for their haste became clear.

He was standing, almost hidden, among the sycamore trees; a sinister, pale grey figure. The last rays of the setting sun glinted across his gold-rimmed glasses, and the lurcher dog, defiantly, it seemed to Ruth, was once again to be seen taking full advantage of the grassy graveyard. She fetched a broom and began to sweep up the flakes of dry brown paint which had been dislodged from her door by Billy and Speedy.

'Hot, this evening,' challenged McInnes.

'Yes,' she replied, feeling foolish and not knowing quite what to do about it.

The dog came towards her; it vaulted the low stone wall, sniffing and grinning, and wagging its stringy grey tail. 'She's taken a fancy to you,' said McInnes, and contrarily, Ruth felt a rare impulsion to show off her new acquisitions. What she needed now, she thought, was somebody to talk to, who was neither a colleague, a criminal, nor a client of Mainstay.

Large as the chesterfield was, she could not bring herself to sit down beside him. Instead, she perched on the small red chair, her long legs stretched out uncomfortably before her. The policeman drank his lager slowly, while his eyes took in the pale magnolia walls and the wine-red curtains.

Ruth studied him, covertly. She noted the highly polished shoes, pressed grey trousers and spotless white shirt. His finger-nails were clean and well-cared for. His face was close shaven. A fastidious man, but not foppish, like Harry. Now he would have probably worn a cravat at his throat on a warm summer's evening.

McInnes. A bony, gangling man; he lacked charm; was surprisingly unprovocative in some areas. He gave off no overt signals: no sexual emanations. To her surprise, she found she could talk quite easily to him. He obviously ironed his own shirts, inexpertly too, leaving several tiny creases at the points of the collar.

'Something wrong?' he asked brusquely.

Aware that she had been staring at him for some minutes, Ruth said, 'No – I, no not really, I was just thinking that you probably have to iron your own shirts these days.'

He shrugged. 'That's nothing new, I always did those jobs. Marion – my wife, she was delicate. From the very beginning.'

Ruth said, awkwardly, 'Would you like to talk about her?'
'No!'

'Sorry, I just thought that – well, it does help some people.'

'Not me. There's nothing to talk about, anyway. She'd threatened to do it, hundreds of times. In the end she did it. Close of chapter.'

'Not quite,' Ruth murmured. 'Nothing ever finishes quite that neatly.'

83

'You should know all about that, Mrs Flemming. You're the "volunteer" lady. The one who solves everybody else's problems.' In the same sarcastic tone he asked, 'Left you, hasn't he? Your husband.'

'Yes, he has. Six months ago.'

'So what in the hell brought you down to this dump? Not' he added magnanimously 'not that you haven't done wonders with it. But it's hardly your accustomed style, is it?'

'I think it's exactly my style,' said Ruth.

'Did you know it was haunted?'

She smiled. 'I can feel it. The spirits are friendly. A young couple and their four children. The little ones patter about in the attic; I can often hear them, late in the evening.'

McInnes looked doubtfully at her. 'You want to watch that sort of thing. This is a damned funny district. Old. Old and creepy.' He pushed a hand through his thick grey hair. 'I've worked here, on and off, for twenty years. Oh, I've had transfers; but somehow, I always land back in St Joseph's.' McInnes looked embarrassed, as if his own thoughts surprised him. 'When you go away from this district – you know – sort of look in at it, from the outside; it's as if everything's out of kilter down here. Out of true. A bit off-balance.' He rubbed his chin, reflectively. 'It's that old church, I reckon; and that ring of gravestones.'

'Is that why you bring your dog there every evening?'

McInnes grinned. 'It's got a certain fascination,' he conceded, 'and it pleases me to see old Sophie defy the local superstitions.'

The distance between them had shortened considerably in the past few minutes. Ruth heard herself saying, 'I couldn't have stayed on in The Mullions even if I'd wanted to. The bank were on the point of foreclosure.'

'How the hell did that happen?'

'Did you ever hear of George Maynard's Limited?'

'Small hosiery factory, down near the river?'

'That's the one.' Ruth sighed. 'It belonged to my father. He built it up from nothing. He left it to me when he died. I made a half-share over to Harry. But the business began to fail a few years ago. The Receiver was called in last April.'

'Well – well,' said McInnes, thoughtfully, 'but why make

your husband co-owner. I get a feeling you didn't altogether trust him.'

'How very perceptive of you,' Ruth said wryly. 'I think I was trying to prove to myself that I didn't suspect him.'

'How do you mean?'

'Oh, you know. The nameless lady caller who would always ring off at once if I answered the phone. The frequent trips he made without any noticeable improvement in business. The way he was never quite "with me" even when he spent time at home.'

'Did you ever catch him at it?'

'No. I never really tried to.'

'Why not, for God's sake?'

'Think about it, Sergeant. He had married me for the money. He owned a half-share in the factory.'

'The house was yours, wasn't it? You could have kicked him out.'

'He came to me with an ultimatum. Raise money on The Mullions, he said, in order to save the business. It sounded reasonable. I knew that a lot of small firms were in similar trouble, and so I agreed.' Ruth looked hard at McInnes. 'Harry didn't go from me empty-handed, sergeant. He took a large chunk of money with him. I've been left to clear up the debris.'

'Debris?'

'We employed two hundred people. They deserved their redundancy payments; most of them had worked all their lives for my father.' She smiled.

'My house was overstocked with valuable antiques and paintings. Fussy, elaborate stuff that I'd always hated. It's been sold at auction, just recently. Every person who had a claim on the firm of George Maynard Limited has been paid in full.'

'And you?'

'I have a small annuity from my grandmother. Harry couldn't touch that.'

She had just told this Detective Sergeant, this aggressive stranger, the kind of secrets she rarely admitted, even to herself. To ease her chagrin she asked roughly, 'What about you, then. What is your situation?'

His eyes flickered briefly towards her, and then away. 'I should have thought the volunteer ladies of Mainstay would know all the gossip.'

Ruth said, 'We're not likely to be asked for help by the families of detective sergeants.'

'Happen not. But there was plenty of gossip at the time. I've never been the most popular copper around these parts. There's always been somebody ready and waiting to shove the boot in.'

'I've heard no gossip about you,' she insisted 'Oh, they say you're a hard man: but that's common knowledge.

'Nothing about Marion?'

'No. Truly.'

McInnes rubbed the heel of his palm hard across his cheekbone. The dog called Sophie looked up at once, from her place on the carpet.

'She cut her throat,' said the policeman, baldly. 'No point in wrapping it up fancy. She made a damn good job of it, did Marion. Ear-to-ear. Used the breadsaw. Just like she'd always promised.' He looked thoughtful. 'There are those in this manor; the riff-raff, and the majority of my colleagues, who will tell you it was all my fault.'

'And was it?'

He shifted uneasily on the chesterfield, and the dog stirred with him.

'My job,' said McInnes. 'I'm no part-time volunteer worker. I don't live in a damn great house up in Hillcrest. Twenty-four hours a day, Mrs Flemming – that's what it takes to police St Joseph's. Even when you're not actually out there, in the middle of it – you're still mentally belly-aching about it.'

'So you had no time to listen to her?'

'Look,' he said softly, 'she had the whole bloody world listening to her. The neighbours – they didn't need to put an ear to the wall when she got started. Then there were the doctors, Christ! She had 'em by the truck-load. She had counselling, psychotherapy, drug treatment, electro-convulsive, in-treatment, out-treatment.' He paused to draw breath. 'They were all listening to her, and what difference did it make?'

Ruth was silent.

'I know what you're thinking,' he burst out, 'that it was me she really needed. Do you think I haven't thought about it –

since she died. Do you think that I don't worry about it?'

McInnes chewed at his lip, breathed deeply, and then continued in a voice grown hard. 'How the hell did we ever get onto this bloody subject. I don't reckon to spill my guts to strangers –'

'Easier with strangers –' she suggested, gently, 'and I'm discreet, Mr McInnes. I never repeat what people tell me.'

'Means sod-all to me if you do.'

'But I don't. You can believe that.'

'You're a funny woman.' He sounded irritable, like a man who had long ago categorised women, and was not about to have his fine theories overturned. He stared at her with those flint-grey eyes, and she knew then how his victims must feel in the local Bridewell. McInnes shifted his gaze to the plain-washed walls and dark carpet. He took in the old brass lamp, the pie-crust table, and the gilt-framed Highland prints over the fireplace.

He shook his head. 'It's a different world in here,' he said, slowly, 'another bloody world, altogether.'

'That was my intention, Mr McInnes.'

He nodded. 'You could be a dangerous woman to know.'

He grinned. 'Stop calling me sergeant or mister, will you? My name's Michael.'

'Michael?' She repeated the word, very slowly. 'Michael is a gentle sort of name. It doesn't suit you. I doubt if I could ever bring myself to use it. Especially in your case.'

## 4.

Friar's Walk was made up of four tall houses and one cottage. As the population had grown and the square expanded, the larger, more impressive houses had been joined on to the cottage: two on either side. Ruth's neighbours were elderly couples, sidesmen and churchwardens; respectable people who 'kept themselves to themselves'. So quiet were they, so unobtrusive, that at least a week had elapsed before she became aware that Number Nine Friar's Walk was empty.

The temperature in the city that day had reached the high eighties, and the setting of the sun brought little relief. At nine in the evening St Joseph's Square still drowsed in a thundery heat. The very trees looked exhausted, and across at the Bird in Hand the vociferous drinkers were unnaturally quiet.

Ruth sat at an open bedroom window: the one from which her view of the churchyard was unimpeded by overhanging trees. She had not seen McInnes; for several days. There had been no word from Georgina since her last visit. But that was her sister's way: to arrive without warning, and to depart as abruptly.

The clock on the tower struck ten. Too late now for McInnes and his lurcher dog to come calling; but still she sat on at the window, absently noting the traffic that came into and went out of, the square. Regretfully, she remembered the beach on Corfu, where Georgina and she had lazed for a month, one summer. There would be no shared holidays in the future.

It was the red and gold shawl that first caught her eye. Much too heavy for a hot June evening. Bizarre in fact, when worn with a long black skirt and the heavy ankle-chains that clanked as the tall girl sauntered through the churchyard. She walked alone in the twilight, carrying one of those big quilted bags made of fluorescent nylon. She should really, thought Ruth, have had a guitar slung across her shoulder. A beautiful, stately girl, with the kind of style that was faintly repellent and a little frightening to a woman like Ruth; a young woman who belonged to a world that most people knew only from hearsay and newspaper headlines. The girl, unaware of her observer, crossed over the narrow footpath that sloped down into Friar's Walk. When she reached Number Nine she paused, and peered in at the uncurtained window of the vacant house. After glancing left and right she gave the sash an experimental shove. Ruth heard it slide upwards, and she leaned forward to see what the next move would be. The girl bunched her full skirts together, tossed the bag through the open front window, and climbed in behind it.

Even in the fading light, Ruth could tell that the approaching van was no ordinary vehicle. It coasted down the little incline and halted underneath the sycamore trees. Painted all over with animals and flowers, it had the sinister bulk and outline of an old-fashioned hearse. Ruth drew back, to watch from behind the curtains. She heard a boy's voice whisper 'Good girl, Cassie.' If she had ever intended to do anything about it, then this was the moment for positive action. Like phoning the local Bridewell, or locating McInnes. But, once again, Ruth leaned further out of her bedroom window, intrigued by the furtiveness of the movements that were going on in the street down below.

The converted hearse held an unbelievable number of passengers. She tried to count heads as they emerged from the wide rear doors. Fourteen souls, altogether, male and female. She could not be quite certain in what proportion, since their clothing and hairstyles were confusingly alike. Guitars figured prominently among their luggage, along with bed-rolls, pots and pans, and a set of drums and bongos.

Once inside the house, with the window closed, and the hearse parked discreetly out of sight close beside the church wall, they were all very quiet. If she had not seen them arrive, she would have sworn that the soft scurrying noises that came from next-door, were the usual nocturnal movements of mice and old ghosts.

McInnes was angry.

He banged on her closed front door on the following evening, almost splintering a panel. Before she could invite him in he had pushed straight past her. For once, he did not sit down, but stood, ramrod-stiff in her kitchen, the cowed dog by his side.

'You knew all about that lot, didn't you?' He jerked his head sideways, towards Number Nine.

Ruth, unaccustomed to outright lying, coloured faintly, and said nothing.

'Bloody squatters! Right next door, and you do nothing to stop 'em. Was it you let them in? Painted bloody great arrows for them, did you?' He almost spat his disgust. 'Lady

89

volunteers; why you're soft in the head, all the lot of you.'

'Why blame me?' said Ruth. 'What could I have done to restrain them, single-handed? The dark girl was in through the window before I had guessed what was happening. The others followed on close behind her. Do you imagine that I could have gone round there late at night, and evicted fourteen people?'

McInnes clutched at his head. 'Fourteen? Oh, my God, so you actually took time to count them?'

'I can't see what all the fuss is about, McInnes. They've got to live somewhere.'

He grinned, without mirth. 'Have you ever lived next-door to squatters? That's a good solid house they've broken into: church property too –'

'Not broken in,' she interrupted gently, 'the sash-window wasn't fastened.'

McInnes shook his head. 'You knew all the time, didn't you? You sat back and allowed them to go in there.'

'But they've got to live somewhere,' she repeated. 'Oh, I know it's not strictly ethical. But just remember McInnes; that we've helped to create this situation, you and I. We've failed these young people; it's your generation and mine who are responsible for this aimless, drifting population of –'

McInnes interrupted, urgently. 'Describe her to me. What does she look like, this girl who came first; the one who brought in all the others.'

'She's tall,' said Ruth, 'dark and slim. Exquisite face: features like a Madonna. It was getting dark, but I could see that her clothes were, well, unusual. But a very beautiful girl. The kind that you always remember.'

McInnes pulled out a kitchen chair, and sat down. He looked drawn, and suddenly much older. 'Did you hear them call her by name?'

'I heard one of the young men say "Good girl, Cassie!"'

McInnes struck the table softly with the palm of his hand. 'I knew it,' he muttered. 'I knew she'd be back here, sooner or later. I just couldn't guess how she'd go about it.' The look on his face made Ruth shiver. 'Do you know who that lovely lass is, Mrs Flemming? That's Cassandra. That's my only daughter.'

Cheese between slices of wholemeal bread; tomatoes sliced thinly. A large hunk of fruit cake, all washed down with lager, and then coffee.

McInnes ate hungrily, hardly noticing what it was she had set before him.

'You've been expecting something like this?' she asked him. She now thought she understood his manic preoccupation with possible squatters.

He nodded. 'After her mother died, Cass disappeared. I had enquiries made, and found out that she was living in a squat, down in Bristol. I went down there, of course. Tried to reason with her. We quarrelled pretty fiercely; she blamed me for what happened to Marion. She threatened to come back to St Joseph's and make life difficult for me.'

'You handled it badly, McInnes.'

'Handled it badly? What the hell are you on about? I should have put my belt across her backside! In any case, what could you ever know about bringing up kids? You've never had any!'

She could feel her face stiffen: feel the anguish twist her features.

'Oh Christ,' he said, helplessly, 'look, I didn't mean to say that. I'd better go. I don't know why I bother to come here in the first place.'

'Yes,' she said softly. 'I was wondering about that, too. Why do you come here McInnes?'

He laid both hands on the table and studied his knuckles. 'I need somebody to talk to,' he admitted, 'who is neither a criminal nor a copper.'

'Don't you have any friends or relatives?'

'No relatives,' he said shortly, 'and policemen don't have friends.'

He had never before, she suspected, confessed to experiencing need. McInnes was the kind of man who would understand what was happening to him, while the psychology of that event would be quite beyond him.

'How old is your daughter?'

'Twenty.'

'Not a lot you can legally do then, is there McInnes, with a young woman of that age?'

'I offered her everything,' he burst out. 'Best schools,

University. Any bloody thing she asked for. I thought we were close. With Marion being the way she was – well, I had to be father and mother; but then she turns round and says the whole damned mess is my fault. Because I'm a copper, she said; because of the way I am.'

The bewilderment in his face touched a vein of pity in Ruth. 'I – I'll try to keep an eye on her for you,' she offered him, recklessly. 'I've got a clear view of next door's garden from my back bedroom window.'

'They've got no right to be there,' he reminded her tersely, 'they're squatters, remember. Illegal occupants of church property. Law breakers.'

'Can't you forget that aspect of it, McInnes. Now that she's back in St Joseph's you might even patch things up between you.'

'Don't be so bloody soft, Ruth! She's doing all this deliberately: to undermine me. Can't you see that?'

In the fire of the argument, he had called her 'Ruth', without even noticing that he had done so. She wanted to go into the sitting-room and be by herself, while she thought about it; but he gave her no chance.

'Just imagine the headlines,' he thundered, 'Detective Sergeant's daughter forcibly evicted from squat.'

'Perhaps it won't come to that,' she said, pacifically, 'if you weren't quite so –'

She abandoned the rest of the sentence and said instead, 'Do you want to see her? You can if you want to; from my upstairs window.'

Ruth hurried ahead of him up the narrow staircase. 'You'll have to excuse the muddle up here,' she said nervously, 'I'm still waiting to have a wardrobe delivered –'

The tableau in the adjoining garden, was, Ruth insisted, unusual only because of the number of young people who appeared in it.

McInnes disagreed. How often, he enquired, had Ruth Flemming seen so many extraordinary looking girls, wearing lengths of wrinkled Indian cotton and swaying mesmerically while half-naked youths in patched denim shorts played guitars.

'Well - no, not in St Joseph's,' she conceded.

'Where then?' he demanded, 'Los Angeles? San Francisco?

92

or some other American city where the degenerates of the world are to be found. Look at them,' he shouted, 'not an honest job between them! Sluts, and layabouts,' groaned McInnes. He turned back from the window. 'She wanted to be a doctor,' he said, 'before she fell in with that lot.'

Downstairs again, seated on the chesterfield, well away from the insidious music, he said, 'I suppose I'd better go home now.' He looked at her, keenly. 'It's no way for a man to live, Ruth. Dragging out one lousy day after another.'

'Perhaps,' she said hesitantly, 'if you could be less belligerent, a bit more understanding. Gentler.'

'Is that how he was – the absent Mr Flemming?'

'No. No, he wasn't.'

'What was he like?' McInnes sounded genuinely curious.

'It sounds improbable,' said Ruth, 'but I don't really know. When he lived with me, I thought I knew Harry. Since he left – I'm no longer sure.' She looked across the room at him, 'All things to all people; that was Harry. A flawed gem: a blurred image.'

All at once, the bulk of the oversized chesterfield in the dark little room, made the space in between them too charged: too confined. Wherever she gazed, the face of McInnes loomed across her vision.

'So what about me?' he asked fiercely. 'How do you reckon me up Mrs Flemming?' Ruth was silent.

'Come on, now. Shame the devil. I can take it! Hard man, eh? That how you see me? Wife-murderer; bad father; rogue copper?'

'No,' she prevaricated, 'not altogether.'

'Yes, you do,' he said flatly. McInnes's face looked exposed, as if she had just scraped the flesh from the bones. 'You're right, of course. How else could I do my job in this city?'

'Other policemen seem to manage it.'

'I've got no room for weakness!'

'There's compassion,' she said softly.

'And what the hell does that mean?'

Ruth leaned out towards him. 'It's going in next door, and asking for your daughter's forgiveness. Never mind the rights and wrongs. You're older and wiser than she is – so make the gesture.'

'I can't do that.'

'Then you'll just have to burn in the fire, won't you, McInnes. I can't help you.'

# 5.

The cottage was old and safe. Once inside it, with the bolts drawn across the doors, she felt cherished. It was as if the house had waited two hundred years for someone like her who would tend and love it. It was only at three in the morning, when the police sirens wailed, and the blue lights flashed, that she began to feel the first quick stirrings of fear.

The fire-engine, the paddy-wagon, half a dozen patrol cars: they were commonplace traffic in St Joseph's Square, after dark. The beat-men patrolled in pairs after nightfall, and Ruth had fallen into the habit of listening for their footsteps every time they passed underneath her window. She did not sleep well since the move.

Up in the Hillcrest district the life after dark had been lived in a decorous manner. People had closed doors quietly, swore softly; and conducted their quarrels in strained whispers, in case the neighbours should happen to be listening in. Life in The Mullions, she now realised, had come gift-wrapped, trailing ribbons.

In the night-time streets of St Joseph's there was no such gentility. The inhabitants of the city jungle raged and roared their frustrations. Fights broke out between relatives: wives and husbands raked up old grievances, and hurled them at one another as they lurched over Ruth's front doorstep. Drunks fell against the wall of her house, and ricocheted smartly away, to lie for the rest of the night in the Friar's Walk gutter. Boys who had not yet learned how to hold their drink, vomited upon the pavements that fronted Dino's café, and the big antique shop. No wonder, Ruth thought, that the unfortunate Italian family were constantly obliged to hose down and broom their stretch of the frontage.

Sam Bright explained the significance of the red and yellow bootlaces that were worn by the local skinheads. Red laces in the right boot, yellow ones in the left, were intended as a signal, said Sam, to all those concerned, that the wearer was a Paki-basher. An enemy of the coloured community.

In the Moslem butcher's shop, the elderly owner, in baggy white trousers and embroidered skull-cap hacked the Halal meat with a bright, thin cleaver. Ruth's mind took a wild leap forward, and suddenly, the possibilities for racial disaster seemed endless.

The West Indian schoolteacher who was Sam Bright's cousin, had said to her, only last week, when speaking of his immigrant pupils, 'They identify with the British – of course they do! Their own culture is not quite real to them: how can it be?

'But don't imagine that their British identity is shatter-proof. It's taken a few pretty hard knocks just lately. Strip them of that, and you leave them with nothing. Then look out for trouble, Mrs Flemming.'

Her establishment in the house in Friar's Walk was finally completed when the telephone was installed, and she needed to memorise her new number. She could, she supposed, have retained her old number; but she did not wish to do so.

There were other links with the past that could not be so easily severed. Just lately, she had begun to worry again about Georgina.

'Danger,' Della Smith warned darkly, across the dregs of the teacup. 'I see danger for you, lady; from a yellow-haired woman.' Since Della's prediction about Edith Hardy's desti-nation had come so disastrously true, it did not altogether do, thought Ruth, to be loose in one's thinking about super-stition. Danger from Georgina had always been a risk when one considered the ambivalent relationship that existed be-tween them as sisters.

With most of her clients Ruth maintained a relationship that was friendly and helpful: but distant. She gave advice on their marital problems (wryly; in view of her personal failure). She tried to counsel wisely in cases of truanting children, insurmountable debt, and inadequate housing.

95

With Della Smith it was all very different. Something in the gypsy girl's make-up evaded the usual routes of human communication. Della either came, like an arrow, to the point she wished to establish; or she insinuated slyly, with such skill, that Ruth was left doubting her own sane judgement.

Each time she visited Nelson Street, Ruth resolved to refuse the offer of tea; and each time she weakened. Della was especially good with tea-leaves. She marvelled, secretly, that this girl, to whom phones and cookers, and the proper care of her children were impossible hurdles, could, at the swirl of a teacup, foretell the future with an accuracy that was frightening.

But it was only a game, Ruth insisted; a charade that was helping the gypsy to feel herself competent at something; and she smiled her disbelief when Della Smith foretold love with a tall, dark stranger.

A blackboard propped up in the Bird in Hand doorway on that Saturday morning, proclaimed in white chalk that there was to be LIVE MUSIK TONITE.

Some drawing power from the next door squatters continually undermined Ruth's purpose. She would resolve to hang curtains, paint a shelf, tidy up her small back garden, and each time the throbbing guitars pulled her back to watch and listen at the rear bedroom window. Seen from high up, they were a busy cheerful group. The occasional altercation broke out about who should go shopping or cook dinner. They always looked hungry, and she wondered how they managed about money. According to Sam Bright, five or six of them sang and played guitar in the local pubs every evening. She had not wished to display too much interest, and enquire whether Cassie McInnes performed in this manner. Ruth thought it was not yet common knowledge that the Detective Sergeant's only chick had come home to roost.

She had not seen McInnes for several days. The presence of his daughter in Friar's Walk had perhaps forced him to find another patch of convenient grass for his lurcher dog? She could hardly remember what he looked like – she had never dared to study his face too closely, feature by feature. To have done so in the restricted space of her small front room would have meant exhibiting an interest in him; one which she was not yet ready to admit. Even to herself.

The MUSIK, as advertised, came drifting across the square soon after opening time. She resisted its claim until dusk came down, and then she capitulated.

The musicians were grouped at one end of the long, narrow bar-room. Four boys and three girls. They had not bothered to dress up for the performance. The girls wore their long drab dresses of Indian cotton, and the boys their brief denim shorts and espadrilles. It was only Cassandra McInnes, in her tarnished ankle-chains and red and gold shawl who caught and held every eye.

Ruth found a seat in a corner among beer-puddled tables and thick blue smoke. A song had just ended, and the frenzied applause and the calls for more brought a satisfied smile to the lips of the singer. Cassie, still unrecognised by her audience as the Sergeant's daughter, was having a successful evening.

The sunburnt boy with the long yellow hair bent his head to the guitar and began to strum softly; and Cassie, never taking her gaze from his face, started to sing in a sweet, rather husky voice.

'The summer days are dying,
The birds are on the wing,
The butterflies are flying,
And I can only sing.'

It was very special; intended for the blond-haired boy and no one else. Each word fell soft and clear into the silence – a love song that never spoke of love.

'The song is all I bring you,
The song is all I have,
The song is mine to sing you,
The sweetest I can give.'

Ruth felt a shift in her mind as if it were the slotting into position of misplaced brain cells. So this was love. A quiet, undemanding song, played by two people.

Sergeant McInnes had been standing just inside the doorway, almost hidden by the dusty chenille curtain. When Ruth emerged into the square he was waiting for her. As she walked towards her house, he fell into step beside her.

It was usually among crowds at traffic intersections, or when standing in line at supermarket check-outs, that she became uncomfortably aware of her height. Walking now with Michael McInnes she was gratified to discover that he was some four inches taller than she was.

'Not wise for you to be out here, on your own, at this time of night,' he muttered, confirming her new sensation of being smaller, and therefore agreeably vulnerable.

She said, 'It was the music that –'

'Jesus Christ!' he exploded, 'do you reckon it worth a mugging to go over and listen to that tripe?'

'I'm sure you're exaggerating the danger,' she said quietly, 'and anyway you were there, McInnes.'

'Just keeping an eye.' He sounded embarrassed.

'She's good – your Cassie.'

'How would you know?'

'It was beautiful,' Ruth said dreamily. 'I've never heard anyone sing like that before; she loves that boy very much, McInnes.'

McInnes was angry. 'Love? Why she looks like a down-and-out whore in that tatty old shawl and those leg-chains, with that band round her forehead.' The argument carried them through the front door and into the kitchen; while the kettle boiled she made sandwiches, absentmindedly. Door-step-thick slices of wholemeal bread with wedges of ham slapped all anyhow in between them.

The music still pulsed in her head. She was conscious of a slackening, a loosening; a slow relaxation of some part of her that had, until now, been buttoned up tight against loving and giving. She sang the words softly, while she buttered bread – 'The summer days are dying...'

McInnes nodded towards the wall that divided the two houses.

'I'll get them chucked out of there, if it's the last thing I ever do. It's bloody indecent. All fourteen of them shacked-up in one small house, together.'

His anger leapt the space between them and lit a fire in Ruth. She pointed the bread-saw at him, 'You're jealous, aren't you?' she cried. 'That's what it's all about, really. You don't care about squatters. Your Cassie's in love with that boy – and McInnes can't bear it.'

They confronted one another across the kitchen table. Suddenly McInnes bent over and deliberately slapped her hard in the face. Ruth lunged at him with the bread-saw, but long before she could nick his smart grey suiting, he had gripped her wrist, and the knife clattered harmlessly among the sandwiches.

'You hit me!' she whispered, astonished.

'And I'll clout you again if you need it.'

She began to struggle, fighting him for possession of her right hand. But McInnes edged his way slowly around the table, and towards her; and she fell back hard against the wall. He touched her face tentatively, with one finger. 'First time I ever hit a woman,' he said wonderingly, 'did I hurt you?'

'Of course you bloody well hurt me!' cried Ruth. 'You almost took my head off.'

He grinned. 'Let me kiss it better, then.' The childish expression, from a man like McInnes, was strangely reassuring. She stood still and allowed him to move closer. She believed he had meant to kiss her gently; but as his hands touched her shoulders, Ruth found herself clutching at him with unexpected violence. McInnes shuddered as his arms went around her. His furious whisper sounded muffled against her neck. 'My wife's been dead for more than a year, now,' he muttered. 'I've not been a promiscuous man – you know what I mean – I'll be bound to hurt you.'

She accepted without surprise what his words implied. She was making important assumptions without conscious thought. 'I've been hurt in lots of ways,' she told him, 'by experts.'

'I guessed as much.' The tone of his voice made her want to cry.

It was hardly the act of love. They had come together through anger, and the fury stayed with them. He left as the first threads of dawn laced the top of St Joseph's steeple. She had half-wakened several times towards daylight, comfortably aware of his bony knee pressed against her spine, or the sharpness of his elbow in her ribs.

At the sound of the door closing quietly behind him, she came fully awake. She stumbled downstairs, moving stiffly and slowly; like a marathon runner who had entered a race that she'd hardly expected to run in, and had not adequately trained for.

Propped up on pillows, drinking hot sweet tea in Harry's

king-sized bed, she felt marginally better. She must, she thought, have been crazy to have invited McInnes to come into her house in the first place. Some women were incomplete without a man. Her mother and Georgina were like that. Ruth had thought she knew better.

Since she never saw herself in the role of available female, she could now be quite certain that she had never shown any provocative behaviour towards McInnes. Yet had she – quite unconsciously – been giving off certain oblique signals, and had the policeman, ever quick to grab at a suggestion, picked up her message, and run with it.

Love-making with Harry, she remembered, had always been a hurried event. As if he had needed to get it all over and done with, before moving on towards something more important. After that first frantic collision of bodies, Detective Sergeant McInnes had taken his time. He had even made her laugh. They had talked about Harry.

'Good lover, was he?'

'Rotten,' she had admitted; knowing, since McInnes, that this was nothing but the truth.

'Good-looking fellah, though?'

'Oh, yes,' she'd said, carelessly. But his angular body had moved away from her then, and she'd said quickly, 'but we never looked right together. Handsome man – plain woman.'

He'd propped himself up on his elbow and studied her face in the amber glow of the street lights. 'How old are you?'

'Forty. Nearly forty-one.'

'So why do you purposely make yourself look so much older?'

'I wasn't aware that I –'

'Ah, come off it. Nobody makes you wear navy blue all the time, and your hair in a bun on your neck.' He'd grabbed at the loose dark hair that spread over her shoulders, and pulled it, hard. 'Get it cut,' he'd ordered, 'and while you're about it, have your skirts shortened.' More gently, he went on, 'You could be magnificent Ruth, if you took the trouble. Why don't you?'

'Because I won't compete,' she'd said, flatly.

The normal span between Saturday and Sunday had been so broadened and deepened by McInnes, that Ruth forgot all about sweeping the paths and the porches of St Joseph's church. It was not until the bells began to peel for the ten o'clock service, that she remembered her duties. She dressd quickly in slacks and an old paint-stained shirt, and crossed over the path to the church.

An assortment of intimate clothing lay about on the tombstones; and a collection of beercans and condoms littered the grass and the pathways. The facility of this broad sweep of lawn was well-known in the district; and why not? After all, she reflected wryly, it was not everyone who had the convenience and the comfort of her king-size bed.

He came back later on that day, walking into her house in full sunlight, caring nothing at all that her churchwarden neighbours, and his own daughter Cassie might see him. She had not expected him back so soon. He had expressed no affection for her. The conventional endearments had not been a necessary prelude to McInnes's lovemaking. No commitment had been given or asked for.

'You all right?' he asked, tersely.

'A bit tired,' she admitted. She did not dare to enquire about his state of health. To do so, in the circumstances, might appear indelicate. Instead, she asked 'Have you had any dinner?'

'I eat later, when the take-away opens.'

'Want a sandwich, McInnes?'

He grinned. 'Good idea,' he said. 'Make me one of your doorsteps.' And then, with no change of expression, 'Why did Flemming leave you?'

Ruth began to cut bread wafer-thin, to slice ham finely. 'I don't really know,' she said carefully, 'he just got fed-up, I imagine.'

McInnes bit into a sandwich and then asked her for mustard. When he spoke again, she thought he sounded tentative, uncertain. 'It's all right then – about last night. You didn't mind – you know?' He spoke as if their night together might have been construed by her as some kind of social gaffe on his part.

'Mind? No. I didn't mind a bit, McInnes.'

'That's OK then. I just sort of wondered if – well you know – in the cold light of day, and all that. To tell you the truth,' he floundered, 'I'm not all that good with women.'

101

'I'm not complaining,' she assured him, 'and if we're telling the truth, I'm not all that successful with men.'

'I'm not complaining either, Ruth – but about your husband?'

'Harry? Don't worry about him. He's gone forever.'

'Man! He must have been crazy, to leave all that he had. That house The Mullions – that was really something.'

'You saw it?'

'Your husband had a lot of valuable stuff up there. He once asked for advice on how to protect it. He showed me all over the house.'

'But you gave me the impression that you'd never met him. Why – you even asked me what he looked like.' She found herself switching to violent anger in less than a second.

'Just checking,' said McInnes, offhandedly, 'I always like to hear all versions.'

'Devious, aren't you?' she gritted. 'It must make life pretty awkward for you, always having to be so suspicious. I don't suppose you ever believe a single word that anybody tells you?'

'There are times when I can't afford to. It becomes an automatic reflex.' With deliberate condescension she said, 'Well, thank goodness I don't need to employ those tactics at Mainstay.'

'Semantics,' he said, disparagingly. 'I've noticed how pretty damn good you are at poking your volunteer nose into other people's business.'

'That's necessary, sometimes.' She was almost shouting at him. 'I have to ask questions, it's all part of the job.'

'Rather like policing, eh? But in a nosy, patronising sort of way.'

She could not remember ever feeling quite so angry. She eyed the bread-saw briefly, and then thought better of it. That particular move might seem calculated to inflame McInnes. Instead, she said coldly, 'Yes – about policing. I've always believed that there has to be something a bit odd about a man who wants to spend all his time harassing and suspecting his fellow humans.'

McInnes said, 'The ones that I suspect and harass can't be classed as human.'

'And what gives you the right to act as judge and jury,

McInnes? That's your whole trouble isn't it? That's what makes you such a twenty-two carat bastard!'

The change in the policeman was instantaneous and dramatic. He gripped her arm tightly, just above the elbow, and propelled her roughly out of the kitchen, and into the little front-room. She sat down in the low red chair, and McInnes faced her. He burned; she could not comprehend so much rancour, such passion. 'Was it something I said?' she enquired.

'Bingo, lady,' he ground out, 'but how did you know that? Oh yes,' he went on, 'I'm a genuine bastard all right.' He bunched his large fist, and studied the knuckles. 'I'm a genuine, twenty-two carat product of Dr Barnardo's.'

'McInnes – I didn't mean to –'

'Oh, don't worry about it. It's what gives me the edge, don't you see. The advantage over people like you. I can be anything I want to; I'm not hampered by coming from a long line of pedigree-stock.'

'Then why are you so angry?'

'People like you get right underneath my skin, Mrs Flemming. You've got the gall to come into St Joseph's and tell other people how to live their lives. You've already made a start on me. Well, I'm warning you – don't try it.'

'But,' she cried, 'I only want to help people –'

'How can you? You're not equipped. You look at everything from the wrong angle. You're on the top of the dung-heap – looking downwards.'

'I'm not!' she insisted, 'I've lost my husband, my house, my money.'

He laughed, without humour. 'Come off it,' he demanded, 'you're a long way from being flat-broke. You're not bumping along the bottom, yet. Not by a long chalk. You still have your bit of private income. Oh, you've come down in the world, Mrs Flemming. But not all the way down.'

'It's only a very small annuity –'

'Small by your standards. You've furnished this place very nicely on it.'

'I had to sell my grandmother's jewellery to do that. Those old-fashioned amethyst and seed-pearl brooches – I had no idea how much money they were fetching.'

'Lucky, aren't you?' he asked drily, 'the way people Will

103

their valuables to you.'

He was making her feel uncomfortable, and guilty. She could hardly be blamed for the fact that he was an orphan.

'You've never had to work for your living,' he went on, 'you've never known what it is to graft for pennies. You can afford to spend time doing anything you fancy: whatever makes you feel good, and squares up your conscience.'

'I suppose,' she ventured, 'I suppose we're both what life and circumstances have made us.'

'With one difference,' he agreed. 'I started out without any pre-conceived notions.' McInnes stood up and moved over to the window. He thrust his hands deep inside his trouser pockets and gazed angrily out at St Joseph's sun-drenched square. 'It was a cold, wet world,' he told her, 'in Newcastle-on-Tyne in the 'thirties and 'forties. Kids like me were always on the outside, with our breeches-arse hanging out, and our noses up against somebody else's window.' He turned round to face her and she could see the pain far behind his eyes. 'I looked around; I asked myself who had the power. I saw the Newcastle coppers patrolling in their warm uniforms, carrying their night-sticks; and by God, that looked good to a kid like me. That's for you, man! I told myself; and so it was. Policing is what I do, Mrs Volunteer Worker. Like it – or leave it.'

'What about your wife; how did she fit into the story?'

'The Chief Inspector's daughter?' he laughed, shortly. 'It seemed like a damned smart move at the time. She was pretty; educated – a real little lady. I thought I was jumping several rungs up the ladder in one go. If I'd been really smart though, I'd have asked myself why a man with the rank of Chief Inspector was so keen to unload his daughter on an ordinary beat-copper.'

'Something – wrong with her?'

He nodded. 'Nerves, they called it. "You'll find she's a bit highly-strung lad," the Chief warned me. What he'd neglected to mention were the six-monthly spells of depression, when she hardly ever washed or combed her hair. There were whole weeks when she wouldn't get out of bed; and crying jags when she smashed the whole house up.' He paused and looked guiltily at Ruth. 'But I never hit her, mind you. I kept the house clean and did the shopping. Shoved poor Cass off on baby-minders. That's another advantage of being a bastard. You don't know what family life feels like, so you don't miss it.' He was silent for some moments, and then he went on, 'It was no sort of marriage though. She was so delicate, and I'm – well, I'm a big bloke. What I needed was a woman I could get to grips with; somebody substantial; like you, Ruth.'

'Well – thanks,' she said drily, 'so glad that I at least satisfy some of your requirements.'

'You don't mind then – about last night?' The recurring uncertainty in his voice dispelled what remained of her anger, and she warmed towards him.

'When I opened my door in Friar's Walk,' she said, 'all kinds of incredible people walked across the threshold.' Ruth hesitated for a moment, and then made up her mind. 'There's something I want to tell you McInnes. I once tried to steal a young girl's baby. Take it from its pram – kidnap it. I was foiled, but the temptation continued, for a long, long time. Since I joined up with Mainstay I don't need to do that sort of thing any more. Do you know what I mean?'

He nodded. 'I think so. But it's no substitute for the real thing, is it?'

## 6.

There had been rumours of racial tension in St Joseph's, as far back as the nineteen-fifties when the first West Indian settlers had arrived. Since then, there had been the odd skirmishes among teenagers; disagreements between Asian and white neighbours. Protests about the siting of the Ram Krishna Temple, or the Mohammadi Halal butcher's business, were a part of daily life. Like the complaints about the strong smell of curry on some streets, and the monotonous chants that marked the yearly celebration of Diwali.

St Joseph's was multi-racial; always had been. There was a synagogue in Crimea Street, a Catholic church just behind the market. The Rastas and the Pentecostals had their established meeting houses; the Moslems and Hindus their temples. The Christadelphians and the Unitarians met side-by-side in identical little wooden huts.

They had all rubbed along together for many years; without very much understanding, it was true, but always with the requisite amount of tolerance and good humour.

But now, the old ways were changing. Ruth had lately noticed an increased police presence on the streets; and she worried about the size of the gangs, both coloured and white, that had started to hang around the cafés and street corners.

She had gone into Waterloo Street at the request of the local Catholic priest. Father Donnelli, while not conceding defeat in so many words, had asked if a member of Mainstay would call on the Ryan family. He had been vague when pressed to reveal the nature of the problem. Mrs Mary Ryan, so he said, was 'a little bit under the weather'.

Mr Matthew Ryan had, rather euphemistically, called his three sons Mark, Luke and John. Identifiable as followers of the present cult, with their shorn heads, baggy trousers and Dr Marten boots, Ruth found the brothers confusingly similar in appearance. They were still lounging about in the living-room at noon, in various stages of undress. Their mother, harassed and anxious, urged one to 'put on some trousers.' Another to 'find a clean shirt.' She implored the youngest boy to 'at least wash your face.'

Mrs Ryan hurried in and out of the room carrying plates of baked beans on toast, and mugs of steaming coffee. The young Ryans, draped negligently over the orange moquette of the three-piece suite, were about to eat a late breakfast.

The family lived in a state of comfortable neglect. Ruth noted a colour TV on the sideboard; an expensive, teak-encased music-centre; a tankful of tropical fish, and a video machine.

'Kids get bored so easy these days.' Mrs Ryan confided to Ruth, 'we get them everything they ask for, but it don't make no difference.' She left the room at three-minute intervals to attend to her sons' demands.

Despairing of ever beginning the interview, Ruth said, 'Perhaps it would be easier if you came round to see me at Mainstay.'

'Ah no, Mrs Flemming, they'll be going out directly. Just as soon as the snooker-hall opens.'

It was the kind of household where the kettle is always simmering on the back burner. Mary Ryan made tea, thick and tawny, a brew that the spoon could stand up in. She pushed the biscuit tin across the table and invited Ruth to 'help herself'.

A budgerigar jumped up and down in its cage; a hamster whirled madly around on a treadmill; a kitten mewed and was promptly thrust into the garden. 'They bring them all home,' Mrs Ryan complained, 'and then leave me to look after them. But pets are supposed to be good for them, aren't they?'

The house and the yard was filled with the clutter of the things their parents had hoped would be 'good for' the young Ryans. Expensive bicycles that had been left out to rust in the rain; TV games that had broken within one hour of purchase. The chairs and the sofa were littered with their fancy leather boots, and belts; their comic books, and multi-coloured clothing.

The placatory tones of Mary Ryan's voice when she spoke of her three children, gave Ruth Flemming some hint of where the problem might lie.

'They're good boys, really,' she murmured. 'It's the company they're into that worries Matt and me. The Father tried talking to them, but it only seemed to make things worse.' She sipped at the scalding tea with a kind of desperation. 'They never go to Mass anymore: and to think – only last year they were, all three, altar-boys at St Margaret's.'

The metamorphosis of the young Ryans from altar-boys to skinheads had been rapid and unexpected.

'What do you think caused it?' Ruth asked.

'It began with our Mark – like always. He's the eldest, where he leads the other two follow. He reads a bit, our Mark does.' Mrs Ryan said this with shy pride. 'Books, you know, Mrs Flemming; and the newspapers. He read this bit about some coloured lads mugging an old lady. It got on his mind.

He kept on about it.' She sighed: 'I don't altogether hold with reading. "Don't be daft," I told him! "You know they're not all like that, you went to school with 'em; why, you used to bring Prem and Dilip home to tea!"'

'What did he say to that, Mrs Ryan?'

'He wouldn't hear it. "It's different now, Mum," he kept saying, "you don't understand about it. There's too many blacks coming into this country. They'll soon be taking us over."'

'And how do you and your husband feel about that, Mrs Ryan?'

Mary refilled Ruth's cup from the big brown teapot. 'As you well know Mrs Flemming, more than half of the houses in this street have been bought up by coloureds: mostly Asians. Matt and me don't dislike them. They're not like us of course. Well, you wouldn't expect it, would you? They've never had all the advantages we've had!' She gazed around with some satisfaction at the expensive muddle of her family's possessions. 'They're very strict with their kids, though: the Asians. I don't really hold with that: nor does Matt.'

'Why not, Mrs Ryan?'

'Well – we come from 'Derry. Years ago now. We was dragged-up, as kids. Never had nothin'. So we bought this house, did it up nice; then we had our three kids. "It's goin' to be different for them," Matt said. So it has been, Mrs Flemming. He works down the docks: I serve in the chippy – part-time, in the evenings. My boys don't need to go out thievin'. "You just ask your Mum," I tell them, "anythin' you want – I'll get it for you."'

Mary Ryan looked outraged: 'Now them Asians, they never let their kids stray far of an evening. They keep 'em close to home, if they can. They take their wage-packets off 'em too, on a Friday tea-time; I've seen 'em do it!'

'Mrs Ryan – don't you think that it might be a wiser –?'

'Our Mark's got no job yet,' broke in Mary, 'he's had interviews; but his dad reckons it's that hair-cut that puts bosses off him. He had such a lovely head of hair, too.'

She reached out a hand across the table, in a whisper she said, 'I'm gettin' frightened, Mrs Flemming. I can't talk to the Father about it.' She dabbed at the biscuit crumbs with a nervous index finger. 'It's our Mark – I'm afraid what he'll do, d'ye see? That Enoch Powell – he was right, so Mark says. Rivers of blood an' all that; running down the streets. Mark's got it in for them Asians just lately; he talks about blowing up their Temple. He don't really mean it – but he's always fed-up; at a loose end, if you see what I mean.' She paused. 'I look at him sometimes, and I think to myself – oh my God, anything could happen!'

Ruth said, 'I could have a chat with Mark, for you. All three boys together, if you'd prefer that?'

'Oh no! That wouldn't do at all. They don't even know you're a volunteer worker. I daren't tell 'em. They think you've come round from the church about fetching some jumble!'

'Well,' said Ruth, 'in that case I can only suggest that you and Mr Ryan try reasoning with Mark yourselves. Point out that violence is no answer to anything. Not having a job will be part of his trouble. I feel sure that this is just a phase he's going through. The shorn head, and the coloured boot-laces are his only way of registering a protest. They don't really mean much.'

The unshed tears in Mary Ryan's eyes suddenly brimmed over. 'You haven't took in a single bloody word I've said, have you?' she demanded. 'They're planning something – I've heard 'em.' Her voice caught on a sob. 'I don't want my three mixed up in it. I'd give all I've got to keep 'em safe!'

'But you can't do that any more, Mrs Ryan,' Ruth said gently. 'Mark is seventeen: he's no longer a baby. We must hope that the values he's learned at home and in church will prevent him from becoming involved in – well, in anything stupid.'

Mary Ryan rested her head in her hands. 'Values?' she asked, 'What use is values any more, in this city?' She raised her head and looked hard at Ruth. 'You bloody volunteer women – you're all useless! There's three cases of typhoid in the Infirmary – I bet you didn't know that! They're bringing disease in the country: that's what our Mark says.' She stood up, looking rather taller than Ruth had remembered. 'I tell you, Mrs Flemming, something's gonna happen round here, before long. Every time I go by the church these days, I have to go in and light an extra candle.'

# 7.

The hairdressing salon was smart: what Georgina would have termed trendy. All wood panelling and cork tiles, with the walls hung with African masks, and fertility symbols; furnished throughout with uncomfortable rush-bottomed chairs. The stylist, a blonde girl in her mid-twenties, wore a gown of dark-blue silk, and was hung about from head to toe with gold. Ruth's eyes travelled down from the three gold chains that swung from the young woman's neck, to eight gold rings – one for every finger. A broad gate-bracelet clasped one wrist, while a laden charm-bracelet hugged the other. There were thin gold rings on several of her toes.

Ruth sat down, and pulled out the metal hairpins that secured the thick pleat of hair at the nape of her neck. 'I want it all cut,' she said firmly.

The girl gasped. 'All of it, madam?'

'All of it. Short all over – like that picture.' She pointed to a pen and ink sketch of a soft, feathery hairstyle.

The girl lifted a tress of the long heavy hair. 'Seems a shame, madam.'

'It's this heat,' Ruth lied, 'I can't stand all this weight on my neck any longer.'

At the first snap of the scissors a pang shot through Ruth and she closed her eyes. It's my old life, she thought sadly, as the swatches of hair slipped away to the floor. She could not bear to watch, but some moments later, she moved her head experimentally, and opened her eyes. Her head felt light; light and curiously empty. The girl still looked uncertain.

'Are you quite sure, madam? I can stop right there if you –'

'No,' Ruth said, 'go on, cut it shorter!'

In spite of her Cleopatra image, the girl was an artist with the comb and scissors. Ten minutes later, she stood back and surveyed Ruth's mirrored head.

'Why – you look quite different, madam.'

It was true. She looked ten years younger. The straight thick hair, released from its burden of weight and length, now curled softly around her head. The shape of her face stood out clearly; and the lobes of her ears, pale from their years of concealment, looked innocent and bare.

The girl grew enthusiastic. 'You could have your ears pierced – and perhaps just a touch of make-up –?'

Ruth allowed herself to be persuaded.

# 8.

She tried to convince herself that the problem of Della, if not exacerbated by too much official interference, would, by some magical process, resolve itself without her aid. McInnes disagreed.

'Look,' he said, 'she's not a professional whore. A quick bang in the jitty behind the Bird in Hand, that's Della's style. But she's picking pockets at the same time. That's dangerous. So far, the men concerned have kept quiet about it. We've had the odd complaint, but couldn't make it stick.' He rubbed his cheek reflectively. 'I'm not so sure about the house. Men go in and out, according to the neighbours, at all hours. When I tackled Evans about it he said they were friends of his, come to talk about business.'

McInnes laughed then, unkindly. 'And you can take that look off your face,' he told her, 'and don't get any broody ideas about that kid, Paisley. Give her another few years and she'll be lifting her skirt, like her mother before her. Kids like her see too much, too soon.'

'No, McInnes! –'

'Don't be bloody stupid, Ruth. You might as well face it. It's what you've been trained to do, for God's sake! What's happened to all your psychology? Your sociological know-how? "Environmental hazard" is the correct term for it, I believe.'

He was right, of course. The whole situation in Number Twelve Nelson Street was becoming a threat; and to the only person who really mattered – the child.

Ruth was finding that her close association with a policeman, was, for some worrying reason, making her more than ever inclined to break the rules. She sat through the Friday discussions of cases outwardly attentive, but inwardly seething. Since moving to Friar's Walk, she had come to resent the restrictions that Mainstay imposed upon her.

Like a demented juggler, she began to toss all her problems from one hand to the other, and high into the air. She prayed that she would be able to keep them all airborne, and within her control.

There was Harry and Georgina. It had taken courage to finally bracket those two together. There was Della Smith and Paisley. Any closer contact with this family would turn her fondness for the child into an unmanageable obsession. There was Jack Hardy, who reeled back to his damp little house in Tulip Fields, every night, uttering threats against Mainstay; and Matthew and Mary Ryan, and their apostolic trio of potential hell-raisers. Finally, there was the atmosphere of St Joseph's itself, which seemed daily to alter. It was not just the July heatwave and its resultant crop of tensions. Something bad had broken loose in the district. What it was, exactly, she could not be certain; but she could feel it. It was in faces, in voices. In the way people looked at, and spoke to one another.

She drove out of the city one evening, without telling McInnes or Imogen Hirst of her intention. It eased her conscience to make these unauthorised visits.

She found the Taylors camped on a stretch of commonland. Three trailers, a brightly-painted lorry, two ponies, a donkey, and the usual pile of rusting scrap-metal; she pulled onto the rutted grass verge, and sat still for a moment. She could feel her heart thumping.

They were perched on boxes and upturned buckets, sitting in a perfect circle, although there was no open fire for them to stoke, on this warm July evening. Three men, four women. All suspicious. All hostile. Ruth walked towards them; a steady walk, slow but self-assured. She'd taken some trouble over her appearance. A white sleeveless blouse, a full, printed-cotton skirt (hemline suitably shortened), a touch of lipstick. She had brushed her short, curling hair until it gleamed, and adjusted the small gold studs in her newly pierced ears. The gypsy dogs, to her great relief, were tethered underneath the trailers.

She came up to the tight little group and halted. They regarded her in silence.

'I'm looking for a Mrs Taylor,' Ruth said, 'a Mrs Kindness Taylor?'

The man who was seated nearest to her spat, with calculated inaccuracy, just managing to miss the toe of her white leather sandal. 'An' who might you be?' he asked; but before she could answer he began to snicker, a wildly unlikely sound from so large a man. 'She'm a big 'un Gran,' he giggled, 'what reckon to her then?'

The old woman raised one finger and the man fell silent. 'I'm a friend of Paisley's,' Ruth said quickly, 'I would like to talk to you about her.'

Without a word the three men stood up. One moved across to the largest trailer and held the door open, while the others linked hands to form a human chair-lift. Swiftly, Mrs Kindness Taylor was transported to her wagon, and set carefully down on an old plum velvet sofa.

It was possible, Ruth thought, to be cautious, so cautious that you caused mischief without being a part of it. The time, she felt certain, had arrived for some very blunt speaking.

'Paisley?' The old woman asked, urgently.

'Quite safe,' Ruth assured her, 'no cause for worry.'

She studied Ruth keenly; the dark eyes huge in the creased walnut face. 'You'm from the Social?'

'Well, yes – in a way. I try to help people who are in trouble.'

'Delilah's in trouble.'

'I'm afraid she is – or at least, she soon will be.'

Mrs Kindness Taylor nodded her head. A well-shaped head, with thin grey hair parted in the middle and twisted into neat little braids, fastened over each ear, with broad amber combs. 'I 'ant surprised,' she said dully, 'I seen a lot o' trouble in my time, lady. But I 'ant never seen one like that Della.'

'You wouldn't consider taking her –?'

'No chance,' Mrs Taylor interrupted. She inclined her head towards the door. 'The men,' she explained, 'the men 'ont let her back, y'see. She'm – she'm – not decent no more.'

'Perhaps – if you talked to her, Mrs Taylor? I've tried several time, but it does no good, I'm afraid. She makes promises, but she –'

'She'm backward, allus was. From a little 'un.'

'Yes,' said Ruth, uncomfortably. 'It's Paisley who does all the –'

'Not right!' The old woman leaned forward, clutching at her long black skirts. 'Not right, that 'ent. Leaving that child with Della! I said so at the time. Give her back to me, I told the Social. Us'll look out for her, proper.'

'It was not my decision, Mrs Taylor.' Ruth looked around her, at the shining brasses, the engraved-glass windows, and the cabinets full of china. 'Paisley ought to be here with you. It's where she belongs.'

''Ent your say-so though, is it lady? Court made the order; signed her over to Della. Nothin' t'be done about it.'

'But she stays with you at the week-end?'

'Aye.' The proud head nodded. 'An' then we hear things. Bad things, lady.'

'Della does try –'

'No! no she don't try! Never did. Bad blood in Delilah. Never be any different. We'm finished wi' her altogether.'

Ruth stood up, careful to bow her shoulders, and keep her head bent, beneath the low-slung ceiling of the trailer.

The old gypsy looked up at her, admiration glowing in her eyes. 'Joss's right. You'm a proper big 'un. 'Andsome figure of a woman, if you don' mind I saying so. Why,' she asked keenly, 'why you got no little 'uns of your own to see after?'

Ruth flushed. 'It just never happened,' she murmured.

'Don' you give up too easy,' said Mrs Taylor, 'you'm a good woman. It's writ in your face. The Lord'll look after his own. As for our Della – don' you fret about that 'un. Us'll look after Della – our way.'

Michael McInnes. Too often in her thoughts, her house, her bed. She got up each morning, bathed and dressed, brushed her hair, dabbed on perfume; shopped for special food and drink – with McInnes in mind.

She tried to convince Della Smith of the dangers of fortune-telling, 'People take it seriously; they believe what you say. Sometimes they act upon it.'

But Della had smiled, and fixed Ruth with that light-green gaze. 'But you wants to know what the future holds too, don' you missus?'

Sometimes she thought about that old trinity of herself, her mother, and Georgina. All her life she had fitted the conventional mould, lived the way they expected her to, acted out the role of the plain, unadventurous elder daughter. There had been pressure. The constriction of one personality bearing down upon another. Talking to McInnes had been like the blowing of a supposedly extinct volcano.

He had mentioned marriage; not seriously, but in the flippant and faintly incredulous way some people discuss their own funerals. He had asked about Harry, several times.

Harry, she had told him, was only what circumstances had made him; like you, McInnes. Like me. There are thousands of Harrys. Grammar School boys with ambitions; articled at the age of seventeen to his father's accountancy business; and bored. So bored, in fact, that life in a northern provincial city had seemed preferable to a job underneath his father's thumb, in fashionable Hampstead. Harry, she told McInnes, had mistaken the trappings for the genuine article. Marriage to Ruth Maynard had not solved his problem. Together, they had settled down underneath her father's roof, only to be marked by the fingerprints of habit. If Harry had found Ruth dull and unexciting – who could blame him?

There was also Georgina. How glibly, she thought, do we assume that because we love somebody, that love is automatically reciprocated. She remembered the morning of her father's death. The visits that had needed to be made to the undertaker, the solicitor, and the Registrar of Deaths. She had virtually forced her sister into going with her; assuming, mistakenly, as it turned out, that Georgina would be glad to perform this last service with her. But now, all these years later, she recalled how Georgina had hurried her along the cold city pavements, and in and out of the gloomy offices which dealt with the minutiae of death.

So patently impatient had her sister been to be done with such unpleasant matters; so unwilling to take her share of what should have been their mutual burden.

## 10.

The storm lasted several hours. Rain had washed the dust from the sycamore trees, and caused a spectacular growth of weeds to spring up in between the gravestones; but it had not, as people repeatedly told one another, cooled the temperature down, but only increased the humidity.

McInnes, like most other people she knew, became irritable in hot weather. 'You could at least leave your tie off,' she told him.

'Can't do that. It 'ud look sloppy.'

'I had my hair cut,' she reminded him.

'That's different; and anyway,' he grinned, 'it's made you look ten years younger.'

He used her house as if it were his own. His comb and razor lay on her bathroom shelf; his dog slept on a length of spare carpet in the corner of the kitchen. Any qualms he might have felt about using the allegedly stolen shower seemed to have been overcome with the onset of the heat-wave. Paisley Smith, who had previously flitted in and out of Ruth's house at all hours, no longer visited there very often.

'I've put my house up for sale,' McInnes told her, one evening.

'Oh. Where will you live then?'

'I don't know,' he said. He looked hopefully at her. When she remained silent he said, offhandedly, 'I'll maybe get a flat. I haven't really decided.'

'What about Cassie?'

'She'll not come back to live with me, she said so; that damned house gets on my nerves.'

'I know,' said Ruth, 'I felt like that after Harry left me.'

'Did you – er – did you love him, Ruth?'

McInnes had stammered over the question. She wished he would allow the subject of Harry some rest; after all, she did not ask, nor had she any desire to be told, about McInnes's wife.

'I loved what I thought Harry represented.'

'That's too deep for me – try again.'

'A home,' she explained, 'a real home, with children in it. Companionship and passion. It didn't seem like too much to ask.'

'And he didn't deliver?'

'I've told you a dozen times,' she said, 'he either couldn't or wouldn't.'

'You sound bitter.'

'I am,' she said restlessly. She sat up in bed, and moved away from his encircling arm. 'Look,' she said, 'if you really want to know all about Harry I'll tell you. But it's quite a long story.'

McInnes reached for a cigarette and lit it. He blew smoke at the ceiling. 'Go on then,' he said, 'I'm listening.'

It took her a full half-hour to explain about Harry. When she had finished McInnes was silent for some minutes. At last, he said, 'Poor little sod.'

'What?' she demanded, 'you feel sorry for him? He had the best of the bargain, let me tell you!'

'Not from where I'm sitting,' said McInnes. 'There's nothing so bad as living with a woman who resents you. If she also happens to hold the purse strings – whew! I don't wonder that he left you.'

'Harry Flemming cheated me,' cried Ruth, 'he let me down on all counts.'

'And what about you?' asked McInnes. 'What did you ever do to make it any better?' He ground out his cigarette-end in the ashtray, and turned to face her.

'I'm not about to sympathise with you,' he said roughly.
'Sounds to me as if you and your father bought a load of
trouble, and then tried to haggle about the price. Your old
man made the same mistake as my Chief Inspector. You can't
buy love as if it were boxed-up for purchase on a supermarket
shelf. But you haven't learned yet, have you?'

'I don't know what you mean.'

'Don't you? This so-called job of yours. You get in too
deeply Ruth. When you're dealing with people – in a place
like St Joseph's – emotional involvement can be a dangerous
indulgence. I've seen that gypsy kid, just lately, in half-a-
dozen new dresses. You're taking away responsibility from
her mother when you do that kind of thing. Can't you see
that you're trying to buy her?'

'The odd cotton dress won't make that much difference,'
she muttered, 'she's made fun of in school, McInnes.'

'So was I. So are thousands of other kids. She'll have to
learn to take the knocks, and the earlier she does so, the
better.'

'It doesn't seem to have benefited you much, McInnes.
You couldn't even cope with your only daughter.'

He dressed swiftly and in silence, leaving her bedroom
without a backward glance. She could hear him stumbling
about in the kitchen, hunting for his shoes. She hoped he
would come face to face with Cassie as he left Friar's Walk; or
the nightly foot-patrol coming from the Bridewell. She began
to recall the past. Harry. The things she had said to him; the
deliberate put-downs. 'Behaviour unconducive to happy
marriage' according to McInnes. Not that he should claim to
be any expert on the subject. 'I'm not about to sympathise
with you,' he had said, 'you can't buy love as if it were
boxed-up for purchase –'

She had never, she recalled, actually sat down and made the
effort to talk to Harry. She had remained mute; had resorted
to silent indignation and resentment. How many times had he
tried to interest her in the business, and she, because it was
not what she needed from him, had refused to co-operate?
She had wanted to hear that he loved her; that he found her
more desirable than her sister.

Georgina. Georgina and Harry. Together. Go on, now
Ruth! Take a good hard look at that picture. No oblique

118

glances; no sideways squinting. Your dark and handsome husband. Your blonde and beautiful sister. But to believe in that brand of betrayal would take time. Ruth would need to grow a new set of bitter lines around eyes and mouth before she could settle for treachery on that scale.

She remembered Georgina's last night in The Mullions. Her feverish agonised searching. 'Where is he?' she had cried. 'Nobody vanishes like that, in a puff of green smoke.'

But they do, Georgina. Oh yes, they do. Ruth got out of bed and walked over to the window. The curtains had been pulled back, and the glow of the orange street lights filled the room. McInnes preferred it like that. 'At our age,' he'd said, 'we can't bear too much illumination.' An honest man, this Geordie. Rude and unflattering; he had also failed to say the words she longed-to hear.


# 11.


Mary Ryan walked into the Interview Room. She sat down heavily in the yellow chair, near the open window, and fixed her gaze on the single pink rose in the bud-vase.

'So you found your way round here?' Ruth asked gently.

Mary Ryan nodded, and then burst out, 'They're goin' to do something bad, very soon now. You got to stop them, Mrs Flemming.'

'Just what do you think they're planning, Mrs Ryan?'

'I don't know. I can't even get to know.' Shamefacedly she admitted, 'I look in their pockets, and their bedrooms. I've thought of all sorts – some of the divils go glue-sniffing down by the railway. But it's not that. They're not smoking reefers neither. The kids what smoke "pot" rub patchouli-oil into their "leathers" to hide the smell; our Mark told me. But there's nothing like that on their clothing.'

'What makes you so suspicious of them, Mrs Ryan?'

She moved uneasily in the yellow chair. 'There's something about them,' she murmured, 'a kind of excitement. Like kids who are off on an outing. For months they were hanging about the house, driving me crazy; now all of a sudden, they're busy. Always in a huddle; whispering.'

'They're just normal boys,' Ruth said easily. 'They'll be whispering about girls, at their age.'

'No. No, it's not that, Mrs Flemming. That copper – McInnes. He had them trapped the other night; he's always walking the streets with that dog of his. Like Matt told him, they wasn't up to no mischief. But that McInnes – he knew better. He's a feller can sniff out trouble. Always could do.'

'I don't know how I can help you,' said Ruth, 'if you can't give me anything to work on. If the boys had already done something wrong – or if you have some definite suspicion?'

Mary Ryan began to cry, 'But why do you have to wait until they've done something wrong,' she demanded, 'why can't people like you prevent things from happening?'

'I want to help Mrs Ryan. Truly I do. Won't you at least let me talk to Mark?'

Mary Ryan wiped her eyes. When she spoke again, there was fear in her voice. 'No! No, you can't do that Mrs Flemming. He wouldn't like that. You see, he's got his pride, our Mark has. It'd look like – well, as if his Mum was fetchin' in the polis' for to take him.' She looked down at her swollen, sandalled feet. 'Whatever it is, it's goin' to be terrible when it happens. Just you remember that Mrs Flemming, when the time comes.'

Something serious was happening. One by one, the lights were springing up in windows all around the square. The sirens were screaming on police cars and fire-engines, and she could see people running. A thick cloud of smoke overhung St Joseph's, and Ruth wondered if she should be out there, too; doing something about it. She estimated that the trouble was probably in Waterloo Street.

She did not go. Instead, she remained at her bedroom window; eyes smarting from the smoke, and her body rigid with a fear she could not name. A nimbus of crimson light spread across the sky, and in its glow she could see Cassie McInnes and the blond-haired boy cross over to the shadowed spot where the converted hearse was safely parked. She had noticed that whenever trouble ran loose in St Joseph's, the squatters made frequent and meticulous checks on their only valuable possession.

The birds in the churchyard trees did the best they could about the dawn chorus. As the first small twitterings struck up, she moved away, very stiffly, from her window.

She went down to the kitchen, moving cautiously in the half-light. She put on the kettle for tea, and made the usual tour of her fortifications; pulling back the bolts, and releasing the Yale locks. By the time McInnes came pounding on her door, it was fully light.

He pushed past her without speaking, and made straight for the bathroom; and almost at once the sound of his agonised retching filled the cottage. She could hear water running, and the noise of McInnes, blundering about, knocking things over. She tapped on the door and asked if he was all right; but he made no answer.

Ten minutes later, he emerged, wrapped toga-fashion in a thick blue bathsheet. His grey hair was dark from soap and water, and he was several shades paler than usual.

'Food?' she asked him.

He shook his head, 'Just coffee.' The sight of his face sent her running for brandy. It was some minutes before she allowed herself to ask him the question that was in her mind.

'What happened, McInnes?'

'Fire. In Waterloo Street. End-of-terrace house, corner of Trafalgar Street. A Bengali family. Mother and five children.'

'All dead?' she whispered.

He nodded. 'The father was on night-shift. The only surviving child is in the Infirmary. He was the lucky one, he's a typhoid-suspect; or so they're hinting.'

'Accidental, Michael?'

'What do you think? A neighbour stated that he saw half a dozen skinheads running away down the street, only seconds before the house went up. But,' said McInnes sternly, 'witness is also a fellow-Bengali.'

She had often noticed that in times of stress, he would tend to speak to her in the curt terms of a police report. Irritably, she demanded, 'So what does that prove?'

'Don't be bloody naive, Ruth. You know the situation. If you don't, then you damn well ought to.'

'What caused the fire?'

'Too early to say, for certain. The fire officer thinks some inflammable liquid – you know – poured in, through the letter-box. The staircase went up like tinder. They hadn't a cat-in-hell's chance!'

'Those boys,' she said, carefully, 'those skinheads. Can they be identified?'

'It was just after midnight.' His voice was weary. 'Anybody on the streets at that time – in this district – will have had a skinful of booze; and anyway, one bald-headed kid looks very much like another.'

He raised his head sharply, then; sending drops of water cascading towards her. 'You know something, don't you?'

'Don't be stupid. I never left my bedroom.'

His tone became suspicious. 'You hear things, in that office of yours. People confide in you. You must pick up hints; bits of rumour.'

'I know nothing.'

'And if you did you wouldn't bloody well tell me!'

He pulled himself up from the table, and walked unsteadily towards the staircase.

When she looked in on him, five minutes later, he was already asleep.


His shoes and clothing lay where they had fallen, on the bathroom floor. She began to sort through them, wondering if anything could be salvaged; and came to the conclusion that nothing was worth saving.

The pale grey suit had been burned in at least twenty places, and even his underwear bore faint scorch marks. The soles of his shiny black oxfords had come loose, and were charred right through. He must, she now realised, have gone into the Bengali house, unprotected. She removed his wallet, a notebook, some keys, and an old briar pipe from his pockets. She would not stop to sweep the paths and the church porches on this awful Sunday.

Walking towards Waterloo Street, in the cool grey morning, she allowed Mary Ryan's words to come back to her mind. 'Our Mark – I know that something terrible's goin' to happen. He's threatened to blow up their temple – remember that, Mrs Flemming. – when the time comes.'

The skinheads had not been recognised. The clothes they wore, the half-mast trousers, the tee-shirts, the single earring, bestowed anonymity on them. Ensured confusion whenever trouble came calling.

The stench, as she turned into Waterloo Street, was overpowering; small groups of women stood about on the pavements. They broke ranks at her approach, and then re-grouped around her.

'Terrible, it were, Mrs Flemming! You should justa seen it. Like Guy Fawkes night, an' that poor woman screaming at the top window! The fireman shouted for her to jump, or throw the baby down. But she just looked dazed. She stood there, doin' nothin' until her hair caught fire, an' she fell backwards.'

The woman who spoke looked ill and shocked. Ruth patted her shoulder and made sympathetic noises; she lingered as long as she dared; but she too, was reluctant to move away from the little knot of neighbours, and walk on to the bitter end of Waterloo Street.

It had been the last house in the terrace. The shocking pink paint on the doors and window-frames was still visible here and there in blistered patches. Through the sockets of the windows a shred or two of unsullied wallpaper fluttered on the breeze. Steam was still rising in little eddies from what remained of the floorboards and brickwork. It was, she imagined, the type of destruction seen in war-zones.

A heat, so intense that it had cracked glass on the opposite side of the street, had subsided now to a comfortable suggestion of warmth. Ruth stood on the ashy pavement and gazed into the shell of the house where six souls had just perished.

Anybody could have done it. Inflammable liquid, McInnes had said. Available to mischievous children; to aggrieved neighbours; to any person black or white, who had seen this particular family as a threat.

Not the Ryans. Please God, not the Ryans. She began to list their advantages. Good home; careing parents; why, only last year they had, all of them, been altar-boys at St Margaret's. They had not needed to pilfer, like the other

123

boys. 'Anything you need,' Mary Ryan had said, 'and your Mum'll get it for you.'

Ruth's head began to ache and she walked slowly away from Waterloo Street, to the Mainstay yard where her car was garaged.

The black leather wallet contained Michael McInnes's address. The bunch of keys held a Yale that must fit his front door. She did not stop to consider that he might object to her entering his house uninvited. To fetch clothing and shoes, for a man who had neither, was a normal, volunteer lady's reflex.

She drove slowly through the Sunday morning streets, looking out for the sign that showed Windsor Avenue. She found it on the very outskirts of St Joseph's. A neat, tree-lined road, filled with red-brick semi's. It was much as she had expected. A tiny front garden: crazy-paving, gnomes. An elevation of stucco, and fake Tudor timbering; a house that looked out of place in this sleazy district. McInnes worked hard at respectability. His net curtains were clean, and his door-knocker shone. The Yale key fitted.

The house smelled fusty, as if he never opened windows or doors very often. Every room had been left in immaculate order; the furniture looked brand-new, still smelling of the cabinet-maker's varnish. It was like a bride's home, or a trendy display in a furniture shop-window.

He kept the house clean. She could not understand his concern, in the circumstances. She remembered her own swift descent into sluttishness, after Harry had left her. McInnes had once stated an aversion to having strangers inside his home, and she thought that perhaps this distaste might also extend now to her. 'No daily woman, poking and prying,' he had said, 'no domestic help – I don't need it.'

He slept in a small, monkish room at the back of the house. His pyjamas were folded neatly underneath his pillow, and a robe of maroon coloured wool hung on a hook behind his bedroom door. She had come prepared, bringing with her a large plastic bag into which she now packed his clean shirts, and the underwear and socks which lay in neat piles in his dresser drawers.

His suits, she discovered, were hung in the large front bedroom. She tried not to look at the rose-ruffled bedspread, but made straight for the wide, double wardrobe. She pulled open the door, and seized the first suit that her hand touched.

Downstairs, in the neat front hallway, Ruth paused while the air settled around her. It was peculiarly painful to be in this house where McInnes still lived; and Marion, his wife, had died. In spite of the summer heat, and the tightly closed windows, it was a cold house. She tried to imagine Cassandra in these surroundings, and failed. There was a sterile look about the gold dralon three-piece, and the smoked-glass coffee tables; and Ruth was not too surprised after all, that McInnes's daughter had preferred to squat.

Number Seven Friar's Walk was a rag-bag of second-hand objects. Treasured books and pictures: all the little unfashionable heirlooms to which nobody else in her family would give house room. Ruth treasured the unlikely: the valueless, the unwanted.

'You've got a knack,' McInnes had once told her, 'of juxtapositioning things just right.'

'Not so difficult,' she had said, 'to position a rose-shaded lamp before a gilt-framed mirror; or warm up a dark little hallway with an old brass tray.'

'It gets more complicated with people. They choose their own spot on the shelf. Look at Billy and Della!'

'Or my Cass and that yeller-haired yahoo!'

'Or you and me, McInnes?'

He had kissed her then, briefly, on the forehead. 'When I was young,' he said softly, 'things came easily to me. Seemed to just happen without any conscious effort on my part. When you get older the machinery slows down. You nudge and position – try to make it happen for you.' He'd grinned at her then, 'I hung about in that bloody old churchyard for hours, on the chance I might see you.'

'No, Michael,' she'd said, 'don't fall into that trap just because you're lonely. Don't choose me, for God's sake. I can't do you any favours.'

# 12.

St Joseph's had always attracted the attention of reformers.
There were more meeting-halls, churches, odd fellowships
and temples around the area, than in any other part of the
city. In recent years the district had also been picked up
briefly, and then put down again by the newspaper and media
reporters. Once again, the fire in Waterloo Street was to bring
the whole world to their doorstep.

Questions were asked in the House by Members of
Parliament who had hardly heard of St Joseph's, and who
would, most certainly, never spare the time to go there.
Something, they said, would have to be done, and done
quickly. Nobody seemed to know quite what action should
be taken; but they all talked a great deal.

McInnes knew what to do. Send them all home, he told
Ruth. Every last bloody immigrant. Every black, brown and
yellow; and all the half-breed shades in between. Give them a
one-way ticket, and enough money to ensure their immediate
welfare. Detective Sergeant McInnes believed in Exodus: on
the grand scale.

Ruth disagreed with him; violently!

Well, she would, wouldn't she? McInnes laughed, genuinely entertained by her naive opinions. He explained to her,
carefully, that she was beset by the usual do-gooders'
syndrome. The compulsion to make the world cosy, to have a
party, and invite everybody in, simply would not do. Life
was not like that, he told her. You first found your own bit of
square footage: and then you maintained your position. You
permitted no encroachment by anybody; no matter how great
their need.

'And are you truly happy, McInnes,' she asked, 'with your
little bit of heaven? With your crazy-paving and your garden
gnomes; your central-heating, and your cavity-wall insulation? Did you ever find love in that rose-ruffled bed? Oh, I've
been there,' Ruth said passionately, 'in that same situation.
Double-glazing won't keep out the sound of the weeping
world, McInnes. Sooner or later, you'll be forced into
listening.'

126

'I know my function,' he told her. 'I slap 'em down when they get rowdy. I lock 'em up when they get out of line.'

'And you enjoy doing that, don't you?'

'For Christ's sake,' he shouted, 'don't you start sorting out my motivation. I had plenty of that sort of argument from Marion. She was the "gentle Jesus, meek and mild" type.'

'And what do you believe, Michael?'

'In getting them before they get me.' He was very angry now. He gestured towards the window. 'I never step out there without knowing that there are a dozen men on this patch who are ready and anxious to slip a knife in between my ribs.'

'I don't know how you can bear to live, like that.'

'Well, some of us have to,' he said, dully. 'I won't make excuses for what I am, or what I do.'

'No. I can see that it wouldn't be wise for you to do so.'

He frowned at her, and then he demanded, 'Well come on then, out with it. Let's hear what you really have on your mind?'

She hesitated, unwilling to bracket hatred and love together; in case one should lean over and contaminate the other. 'I want to love you, McInnes. Ridiculous isn't it, at my age?'

'I'm not a loveable man. I don't ask for it. I don't need it.'

'You want Cassie to love you.'

'That's different. She's my daughter.'

'No it isn't. Love is love; it's being able to accept the whole person, warts and all.'

'And you can't accept me?'

'Not as you are.'

'I can't change.'

'I already guessed that.'

'It's good in bed, Ruth.'

'Not enough McInnes. Not for me.'

'It's more than you ever had with Flemming. You said so.'

'I know,' she moaned, 'that's the trouble. I've become greedy. I want it all.'

He shook his head. 'Sweet Jesus,' he muttered, 'I certainly know how to pick 'em. Marion was a raving neurotic, and now you – you turn out to be some sort of pacifist freak who can't love a man because he's a copper.'

127

'But you don't want love – you just said so.'

'I wouldn't know what to do with it,' he burst out. 'Back off Ruth, if you value your safety – back off me!'

Allowing her thoughts to edge forwards, meant that she must also reach back; so that thinking about Michael McInnes became synonymous with recalling Harry Flemming. It all came down in the end to deciding what really counted, and cleaving to it.

'Don't be so bloody trusting,' Georgina had told her. 'Look at you, forty years old, and still taking people at their face value. People are rotten, Ruth. All of them. No exceptions. All grinding their own little axes. All working out what's in it for them.' Ruth had not believed her.

It still pained her to admit that Harry had deliberately tricked her. It would have been easier if she could have viewed her husband from a standpoint of unfocused, romantic regret. Which brought her back again to McInnes. Her feelings about him were not unfocused; but regret existed, and a vaguely romantic aura of which she felt slightly ashamed. It did not do to feel gauzy about a man like Michael.

'This place,' she'd told him, 'it's a war-zone. Religion against religion. Colour against colour.' She had pointed at the skyline. 'Look out there. Church on the one hand, and Bridewell on the other; and standing in the middle is Mainstay and its handful of bumbling do-gooders.' She had smiled then, at the surprised look on his face. 'Oh yes; I've come round to your way of thinking. I once believed that what I was doing here had some value. Now I just see myself as a repository for other people's secrets. Do you know what they say to me? They say; "I can tell you can't I, Mrs Flemming? I could never tell this to anybody else – but I know I can trust you." But the secret, once imparted, is the barb that skewers my conscience, Michael. You were right – you and Sam, and Georgina. I am over-involved.'

'And what about us, Ruth. What about our involvement?'

'I've heard stories about you, McInnes. I've seen the way you operate on the streets. They say that you can beat up a man without leaving any bruises. That you have a knack of humiliating a suspect so that he's never quite the same after coming into contact with you.'

He'd shrugged. 'So I take a hard line when I need to. But I'm handling thugs, God damn it! I've got a certain reputation – I won't apologise for it. You don't like it; neither did Marion, nor does Cassie. Do you think I feel happy about that? People like you Ruth; tranquil people who have beliefs, you're a pretty rare breed. So rare in fact, that a man like me will do almost anything to keep a woman like you alongside him.'

'Except alter?'

He'd sighed. 'I'm fifty next birthday. It's too late now.'

What was it about McInnes that made her so unwilling to give up on him? There were times when her dislike of him bordered upon hatred. He seemed to have a knack of bringing out the worst and the best in her. She wanted to take him apart and re-arrange him. But if she did that he would no longer be McInnes.

She sat in the dim little sitting-room that overlooked the churchyard; the room she had coloured magnolia and crimson. Her books, her pictures, her tiny porcelain collection, should all have left her own thumbprint upon it. But the room now belonged to Sophie and McInnes. His spare pipe and matches lay in the ashtray, and the moulting lurcher had left tufts of her soft blue hair on the carpet. McInnes and his dog had been subtly invasive. He rarely slept any more in that monkish bedroom in Windsor Avenue. His pyjamas were permanently underneath her pillows; and his maroon woollen robe lived on a hook behind her bedroom door. They made use of one another.

She went back to Waterloo Street on Monday morning. Matthew Ryan opened up to her knock, drawing back bolts and releasing chains, as if his was a house under siege.

'Can I come in?' she asked him.

'The wife's not here.' He continued to stand in the half-open doorway. 'Message came late last night from the sister in 'Derry. The ould mother's bin' took queer-like. They said for Mary to come right away. She got the first ferry.'

'I'd like to talk to your sons,' Ruth said firmly.

Matthew Ryan studied his feet, and then looked up at her. 'They went with their mother. Well – they hadn't had a holiday for ages –'

'I see, Mr Ryan. So they're all four in 'Derry?'

'That's right ma'am,' he seemed relieved at her easy acceptance of his story, 'they'll be gone for awhile yet.'

As she started to walk back towards her car, Matthew Ryan called out in a high, penetrating voice, 'Your fancy-man was round here, not half an hour since. He was asking questions. I've told him the same story as I've told you.'

She heard him bang his door smartly; and she winced at the rap of the bolts as he slammed them hard home.

The next intimation that roles might have been reversed, and tables turned, came from Paisley. At sight of Ruth, the gypsy child slid from the room, without a word, eyes averted.

Della, on the other hand, was uncommonly welcoming. 'Come you in, now missus,' she cried, pulling up a chair. 'You just sit quiet for a sec while I put on the kettle.' When she returned with the tea Della said, 'You lookin' tired, missus. Too many late nights eh?'

'I don't think so,' Ruth said stiffly. 'How are you, Della? Any problems?'

The expected litany of unpaid bills, hostile neighbours, and the shortcomings of Billy Evans, was to be abandoned on this occasion for more gripping topics. 'You had your hair cut!'

'Yes. It was the heat,' Ruth said quickly.

'An' after all them years it must have took you to grow it!' Della sounded scandalised. 'O' course, some fellas like it short, I know.' She glanced at Ruth from beneath sly, half-closed lids. 'Billy likes me to have long hair. He reckons it's sexy.' In the same knowing voice, she went on, 'You've bin havin' it off wi' that copper, an't you? Not that I blame you!' Della made haste to reassure her. 'I made him the offer meself, but the cheeky sod said he was a bit more pertickler than that. You watch out for him, rawnie! He's a wicked old bastard, that McInnes.'

Ruth could feel the hot colour flood into her face.

'Don' you worry.' Della was determined now, to set Ruth at her ease. 'I know how it is when you gets lonely. Like Billy said, it jus' shows you the "social" is human, like anybody else.' She slopped tea into a mug and handed it over. 'But don' you let that McInnes get the upper hand,' she counselled. 'You keep him guessin'. That's what I do.' Della wriggled ecstatically in her armchair, and giggled. 'Some nights, when I really wants to get Billy goin', I lock the front door. "Let me in darlin," he shouts down the keyhole, "come and see what I brought you." "I know what you brought me, you randy little toad," I shout back. O' course, I have to let him in later on. Well, the neighbours get stroppy about all the din, don't they?' Della nodded. 'You play it cool. It works a treat. Every time.'

When McInnes arrived that evening she was seated, uncomfortably erect, in the small red chair. He patted the chesterfield.

'No,' she said, 'I'll sit over here. I want to talk, and I'll need to look into your face while I do so.'

He took out a cigarette and lit it. 'Sounds ominous. Just don't try psychoanalysing me, that's all. It's too damned hot – and it's boring.' He drew smoke down into his lungs, and then blew it, provocatively at her.

Into the silence, Ruth said loudly, 'We're ridiculous, McInnes. Have you ever thought about that?'

He looked wary. 'Hang on. Take it slowly. You're at it again, aren't you? Trying to confuse me with your half-baked Freudian theories.'

'Oh, shut up!' she cried, 'and listen for once in your life. I'm serious, Michael.'

'What's happened, Ruth?'

'People.' She almost sobbed. 'People know all about us. You and me. Together.'

He lifted an eyebrow. 'Co-habiting?' he asked lightly. 'So what of it? Nobody's business but our own.'

'You seem to forget I'm a respected member of this community. I work for Mainstay.'

'Took a vow of chastity, did you? Promised not to get into bed with horny policemen?'

She blushed. 'You know what I mean, McInnes. It's – well, a question of ethics.'

'Ethics? That's rich my lady, coming from someone like you. You, who could swallow a stolen bathroom suite without a hiccough? You know something about those Bengali deaths in Waterloo Street, but you're not letting on. You withhold information from the police, Ruth. You

131

condone immorality and crime on a scale that I'd never have believed possible. Look at Number Twelve Nelson Street – that gypo has sweet-talked you into letting her set-up a knocking shop, down there. That kid Paisley – why every shopkeeper in the district nails his goods to the counter when he sees her coming.'

He paused, and stubbed out his cigarette. 'Ridiculous, you said. You and me together?'

'We're middle-aged, Michael. Not permissive teenagers. We don't equate with the next door squatters. It's too late for us. We're too firmly fixed in our respectable niches.'

'Speak for yourself,' he said roughly. He swallowed hard, 'I'll – I'll marry you, if respectability's what you're after.'

'You'll have to stop coming here.'

'Meet elsewhere you mean. Like at my place?'

A shudder ran through her. 'No. Not at your house. Not anywhere McInnes. I mean finish it. Altogether.'

His eyes gathered up the room, coming last of all to the square gilt mirror that reflected St Joseph's square. 'I don't think I can do that,' he said bluntly. 'You're a bloody hypocrite; you didn't give a hoot about ethics just as long as you weren't found out. You've enjoyed going to bed with me, now admit it!'

'No, I haven't,' she lied, 'in fact to tell you the truth McInnes, you're beginning to disgust me.'

He stood up and snapped his fingers at the sleeping dog. 'Come on girl,' he muttered, 'we'll be getting home now. Looks like we just outstayed our welcome.'

*Part Four*

# AUTUMN AND WINTER

# 1.

Her sister, it seemed, had not lost her uncanny knack of materialising whenever Ruth found her emotions in a state of flux. Rather like a slumming duchess, the long white car slipped self-consciously into position behind the flower-spattered hearse, and Georgina, elegant in green linen and Gucci sandals, stepped out into Friar's Walk on a cloud of Arpège.

Ruth deliberately avoided the usual, effusive greeting.

'You've changed,' said her sister, later on that evening, 'and it's not just the hairstyle and earrings, and the revelation that you have stunning legs. It's your whole damn persona.' She laughed, uncertainly. 'I don't know that I like it, Ruthie. You've become decisive.' Intuitive as ever on such matters, she asked, 'Who's the man, then?'

'He's hardly your sort, Gina. He's a policeman.'

'But that's marvellous darling! I've always seen you as a "Dixon of Dock Green" bride.'

'Oh no,' Ruth said gently, 'this one's a swine. Everybody hates him.'

'Well, you always were perverse my dear. Is he married?'

'Widower. According to her father, his only daughter is

chief rabble-rouser in the next door squat.'

'But how deliciously squalid, darling! Personally, I'd find it quite a turn-on. But I'd hardly have expected it to have that effect upon you.' Without any change of tone she asked, 'Where's Harry Flemming?'

'Why do you keep on asking me that question?'

'Do you really not know, Ruth? My God,' rasped Georgina, 'women like you make me want to vomit. You're so bloody trusting it seems almost impolite not to take advantage of you.'

'And how far have I pushed you and Harry in the cause of good manners?'

'Pretty far.' Her shoulders slumped and her eyes filled with tears.

'Do you know what he did? He left me asleep in a crummy motel room just off the M1. He took off in a raging blizzard; it was so unlike him. He'd developed a cold and you know how he worries when that happens.'

Ruth smiled, 'Harry would probably have had a ticket for Barbados or Bermuda in his pocket. You really didn't know him any better than I did, did you Georgina?'

'Oh, I knew him. I just never credited him with sufficient spirit to double-cross me. After all, it was my idea that he should persuade you to borrow money on The Mullions. He was too damned slow to think up a scheme like that on his own. I remember your wedding.' Georgina leaned her head against the red velvet chair, and closed her eyes. 'There was Father, looking stuffier than ever. Mother in her lavender chiffon mother-of-the-bride outfit; and you, Ruthie! Whatever had inspired you to choose a full-length dress of white crushed-velvet? You looked exactly like an elongated snowman.' She smiled and opened her eyes. 'And then I saw him, the bridegroom; standing there beside you; and I simply could not believe my eyes.' Georgina leaned forward in her chair, 'My God, but he was gorgeous, Ruthie; and do you know what made him so incredible, so bloody irresistible? He didn't even know the effect he had on women. He was actually a shy man.'

Georgina examined the varnish on her fingernails; tapped crimson upon crimson. 'Since I was not a complete bitch in those days, I stayed away from The Mullions for quite a long time. Until Father died, in fact. I came up for the reading of the Will. Remember that day, Ruthie? But of course you do. That was the day you claimed your birthright. The day you finally hit the jackpot. It paid off in the end, didn't it? All that sitting up at night in the sick room; mopping Daddy's chin when he dribbled his soup; emptying the bedpans.

'To my beloved daughter, Ruth Alice Flemming – so that she may, before it is too late, experience freedom.' Georgina smiled. 'It didn't work though, did it? Father had got his sums wrong. Money was not what you wanted, and there was your Harry. A little heavier, a little broader in the shoulders, but still, in spirit at least, a virgin. Oh yes, Ruth! That's what he was. It took me precisely two minutes to find that out.

'You had the house, the factory, the money, but by God! I had your husband. In your house, in your bed. He was never quite the same man again, was he Ruthie? Or perhaps you never noticed? If I remember correctly, it was about that time you began to go all broody, and started moping about the place, hankering for a baby.' Georgina laughed, uneasily. 'Harry Flemming cheated us both, in the end; and perhaps we deserved it.'

## 2.

She had never consulted Dr Fowler on her own account. She had corresponded with him on behalf of clients; and they had met briefly in the courtroom, at Edith Hardy's inquest. Ruth felt embarrassed, and slightly fraudulent at taking up space in the crowded waiting-room, with no more to complain of than an upset stomach.

'What's the problem?' He seemed surprised to see her.

'Just generally out of sorts, doctor. Nauseated, and giddy.'

'It's this damned heat,' he said comfortably, 'you've been overdoing things I expect.'

'I don't think so.'

'How old are you, Mrs Flemming?'

'Forty-one tomorrow.'

'Tell me more about it.'

She told him.

'Is there any possibility that you might be pregnant?'

'Oh, no,' she said decisively, and then, 'Well – yes, I suppose so.'

'Have you any children?'

'No. I was told – several years ago – that I was not likely to conceive.'

'I see. Of course, it's highly unlikely at your age. I'll do some tests: set your mind at rest, shall I?'

As soon as the doctor had voiced his suspicion, she knew that it had to be the truth. Nothing else would explain her recent difficulty in fastening skirts and blouses, or the other discomforts she had experienced. She went back to the surgery three days later.

'What do I say to you, Mrs Flemming? Do I congratulate or commiserate with you?'

'I think you congratulate me, Dr Fowler.'

'Are you certain? There are risks at your age.'

'I was a nurse before I married.'

'Then you'll be aware of the dangers.'

'I've wanted a child for so long –' she said, simply.

'How does your husband view the prospect?'

Hastily, she reassembled an almost forgotten Harry. 'Oh,' she smiled, 'he'll probably find it hard to believe when I tell him.'

A letter arrived from Georgina. Her sister had written, part in apology, part in justification. 'The trouble between us has always been your profound morality, darling. I think it might be wiser if we don't meet in the future.'

She had never been quite alone, before. In the past there had always been her father and mother; and Georgina.

Ruth lay awake in the over-sized bed and heard the church clock strike the quarter hours. She counted up the doors which, because of association with McInnes, had now been closed tight against her.

Her departure from Mainstay was inevitable. She could,

she believed, rely on Sam Bright for support. Of Imogen Hirst she was not so certain.

She thought about her mother, living graciously in her Italian flat; neatly cut off from her daughters by style and space. It would hardly be kind to announce her first grandchild; conceived out of wedlock and fathered by a policeman. There was another, more sinister reason for concealment.

Mrs Maynard had only ever involved herself in those situations which promised her power, and news of Ruth's plight might well bring her running, laden down with expensive, useless gifts and determined to control the whole operation.

This child was to be Ruth's sole and private project. If she tried hard enough, she might even succeed in believing that she had suffered an immaculate conception. Resolutely, she attempted to tamp down all memory of those torrid summer nights she had spent with Michael McInnes. Number Seven Friar's Walk, she decided, would become a fortress; and the wronged maiden would await the birth of her child alone, and with as much dignity as St Joseph's would allow her.

News of her pregnancy was accepted in various ways, depending on the tact of the recipient. Imogen Hirst chose, diplomatically, to credit Harry Flemming with the miracle: she assumed his flying-visit to Friar's Walk on a mission of reconciliation; and Ruth did not disabuse her.

With Sam Bright it was different. He sat at her kitchen table one Sunday morning, drinking coffee. 'I'm leaving Mainstay,' she said, abruptly, 'I'm pregnant.' He set down his cup very carefully into the saucer, and then asked her the question she had not dared to ask herself. 'Do you want a child by McInnes?'

'I want a child, Sam.'

'Child has also got a father.'

She knew what he meant, and just for a moment she felt frightened.

'Anything you want, Ruth. Anything I can do for you. Just say the word.'

Sam's concern was uneasy but kindly.

'I'll be all right,' she insisted, 'I've worked it all out.'

He went away; and now she began to evaluate the precise contribution that was brought to a child by its father. Ruth foresaw a miniature McInnes, and baulked at the thought. Suppose, at the end of it all, she did not even love the child she had borne?

It was possible. She had seen it happen. One of her earliest clients, a thrice-divorced mother called Netta had complained of her son from a former marriage. 'I can't seem to take to him, Mrs Flemming, really I can't. He's not like the others. Ronnie's weird. He does weird things.' Netta had been unable to explain in what way Ronnie was different, but Ruth suspected that the child might resemble his rejected father.

She thought about the girl who already called McInnes 'father'. Cassie, sleeping tranquilly in the next door squat, became a source of comfort to Ruth in the long night hours when she could not sleep. McInnes no longer saw his daughter as a child he could be proud of; but Cassie was capable of love. She made her own judgements and held to them. Her return to St Joseph's had not, as her father predicted, been made solely to disgrace him. The next door commune lived quietly, troubling no one. Perhaps Cassie McInnes had only wanted to be near her father? She might even long for a reconciliation with him? People sometimes needed one another without knowing it.

The end of October, and St Joseph's square was coloured in russet and dun. The last leaves fell, and sycamore keys whirled down the wind to fetch up in a silvery drift all around her doorstep. McInnes and his dog came to see her.

'I see you've bought new lampshades,' he observed, looking everywhere but at her.

'And I've had bookshelves built in. I plan to do quite a lot of reading this winter.'

'Very nice.' He glanced nervously at her thickening waistline, and then quickly away. 'You can't do this to me Ruth,' he muttered.

'Too late, McInnes,' she said sweetly, 'who told you, anyway?'

'It's all round the district.' He looked troubled. 'Nothing's private in this place.'

'But you were the one who never worried about gossip,' she pointed out.

'What will you do about Mainstay?'

'I'm only a volunteer,' she reminded him, 'and as you've so often remarked it's a job of very doubtful worth.'

'And afterwards?'

'I'll go back to nursing, if I need to.'

'Got it all lined up, haven't you?'

'Don't forget,' she said, 'that I've been trained to deal with these sort of situations.'

McInnes brooded. 'Have you thought that by the time this child is twenty, I'll be seventy.'

'Ah shame!' she said smoothly, 'he can push you round in your wheelchair.'

'You're no spring chicken, Ruth. Childbirth can be risky at your age.'

'Anything's risky at my age. Opening my door and letting you in was the first wild chance I took.'

'Do you regret it?'

She shrugged. 'I'll let you know about that – next May.'

'I – I'll look after you, Ruth,' he said hesitantly. 'I've been thinking it over. We'd better get married.'

'I've already got a husband.'

'Divorce him.'

'I don't know where he is.'

'I can find him for you.'

'No Michael.'

'Why not?'

'I'm not sure,' she said thoughtfully, 'that you're quite the sort of man I really want as a father for my child.'

'For Christ's sake!' he exploded, 'it's a bit late in the day to find that out.'

'Yes, I know.' She laid a hand on her stomach. 'It's been bothering me lately. Genetics, you know. Inherent tendencies, and all that.'

McInnes looked bemused. 'I don't believe I'm hearing all this. Why – even my unborn child isn't safe from your daft psychological claptrap.'

Ruth turned slowly to face him. 'Let's get something quite clear, McInnes. You have no claim on this child. Push me too far and I'll deny you're the father.'

Behind the gold-rimmed spectacles, she could see his eyes widen. 'You can't do that; make private arrangements with yourself. I have rights. I shall need to be consulted.'

'No, you don't,' she said firmly, 'and already we're fighting about hypothetical cases. I won't tolerate that, McInnes.'

He tapped his chin, uncertainly. 'You've changed.'

'It was about time,' she said. 'Immaturity sits badly on a woman in her forties.'

'I don't go in much for thinking, Ruth.'

'I'm sorry.' She leaned forward impulsively and covered his hand with hers. 'I'm sorry to force you into fatherhood at this late stage, and against your will.'

'It's not that simple,' he fixed his eyes on the sleeping Sophie. 'I told you about myself – how I never knew where I came from.' His voice grew rough. 'Kids need a father. I can only remember the rain and the cold when I was little. I did no better by Cassie. She was pushed out all week to a baby-minder.' He paused, 'How the hell could I have done that to her?'

'Not your fault,' Ruth said, unsteadily, 'you said that your wife was unstable.'

'But you're not, are you? You're a very tough lady; you're the strong one.'

'No,' she said, and this time the tears spilled over. 'Don't see me as a second chance, Michael. I want to be on my own. I don't need you.' McInnes had never seen her cry. Perhaps he had thought that she had no tears.

'Oh, Christ,' he moaned, 'I've got it wrong again. First with Marion. Then with Cassie. Now, worst of all, with you.'

'Why worst of all, with me?'

The bewilderment in his eyes deepened. 'Something's happening to me, and I don't much like the feeling. Happen you're right, after all,' he said, 'happen I should stay away.'

# 3.

On a bitter night in December she opened her door to Jack Hardy.

'Can I speak to you for a minute, ma'am?'

'Are you sober, Mr Hardy?'

'As a judge.'

He sat in the small red chair. 'I just wanted you to know,' he muttered, 'that it weren't your fault. About Edie, I mean. That bloody gypo filled her up with a pack of lies. It's been on my mind a lot lately.' He glanced at her altered outline. 'Me an' Edie shoulda' had kids,' he said sadly. He coughed and looked embarrassed. 'I heard about your bit o' trouble, Mrs Flemming. If there's anything I can do to help you, you only got to say the word.'

'That's very nice of you,' Ruth said warmly.

'No. I really mean it. How about letting me paint your front door and windows. There's hardly any paint left on 'em.'

Jack Hardy came back at the week-end with his brushes and ladder. He painted her window frames white, and the door a deep shade of blue. Over bacon and eggs in her kitchen, he confessed, 'I can't give up the drink altogether. I still go to the pub every evening. I can't stand being in that bloody house by myself.'

'Have you thought of moving out, Jack?'

He laid down his knife and fork. 'Matter of fact, I have. Thought a lot about it, just lately.'

'Then why don't you –?'

'Don't seem fair to Edie. As you well know Mrs Flemming, it was all she ever wanted. If I was to flit now she's gone –'

'I think she'd understand, Jack.'

He looked at her oddly. 'Believe in that sort of thing, do you?'

'Yes, I do.' She hesitated. 'Why don't you go home and talk it over with her; tell her how you feel?'

'Out loud you mean? As if she were still there? I'd feel bloody daft, doing that.'

'No, you wouldn't. I often talk to the ghosts who live up in my attic.'

Jack Hardy shivered. 'It's living on your own that does it, ma'am. Starts to send you funny in the end. If folks was to hear me talking to Edie I'd be put away.'

'The world is full of lonely people,' she said, 'you may find someone else to share your life with, at some time –'

'Don't always work out right, though does it?' His pale face reddened. 'You want to hold out for marriage Mrs Flemming. Folks reckon that pig McInnes owes you that much!'

Early morning frost made each blade of grass stand up white and straight in the churchyard. She laid in a stock of coal and logs for the open fire; planted daffodil bulbs in the small back garden; and made secretive plans to position the pram underneath the pear tree, when spring came. Her retreat had been gradual, to begin with; but now, with the onset of winter, her world shrank within the frame of St Joseph's Square and her own tight cottage.

The Mini was an extravagance she could well dispose with; and so she sold it and went shopping with the money. She bought a loose-fitting woollen coat in dull orange, smart suede knee-boots, and a dramatic hat of spiky brown fur. People who had known her for years did not recognise her.

She felt especially unreal in the early mornings. The sounds of people passing through the square on their way to work only pointed up her own lack of incentive to get out of bed, and begin another day. This was the time, she told herself, to draw comfort from the cottage. To lock the doors, light the lamps, and build fires against the winter. Mary Crofton too often pregnant, and with little hope of bearing a live child, must also have known the same doubts and fears.

Nothing was certain; nothing had been promised to her. She felt that her whole life was about to unravel, stitch by stitch; all of it pulled loose now, just lying slack between her idle fingers.

On Christmas Eve McInnes brought her presents. A miniature tree hung with stars, chocolates, and a voluminous robe of soft, apricot silk.

'I haven't got anything for you.'

'I can wait,' he grinned, 'until May.'

144

'You won't bribe me with dressing-gowns and Christmas trees. Why don't you stay away McInnes, like I asked you to?'

'I've sold my house.'

'Oh yes.'

'Don't you want to know where I'm living?'

'I expect you'll tell me.'

'I've got a flat in Crimea Street – just around the corner.'

There were other presents that Christmas. Billy Evans and Paisley appeared on her doorstep. They carried an unwieldy parcel wrapped up in brown paper. Billy handed it over, saying swiftly, 'I made it meself ma'am. I hope it's OK.' She invited them in, but they made excuses; and she watched as they hurried away through the square, heads bent against the cold.

Billy Evans had lovingly carved out a perfect replica of the ancient rocking cradle that was presently displayed in the antique shop window.

On a bright, cold day in March she came face to face with Cassandra McInnes in St Joseph's market. 'Carry your shopping, Mrs Flemming?' asked the policeman's daughter. Cassie's face, that smooth Madonna-oval held a curious expression, half-defiant, half-pleading.

Ruth relinquished the heavy bags to her, without a word, and they strolled back to Friar's Walk together. When they reached her door, Ruth said, 'Would you like to come in? I could make us some tea.'

McInnes's daughter sat cross-legged on the hearth-rug, and toasted scones, on a long-pronged fork. To Ruth, in the seventh month of her pregnancy, such slim, athletic beauty seemed the only desirable state in which to be, at that moment. Cassie stared at her, frankly.

'That's my father's child, isn't it?' It was a statement, made as easily and calmly as she might have announced that it was raining.

'Yes,' Ruth admitted.

'How does he feel about it?'

'I think you'd better ask him that question.'

'Are you getting married?'

'I don't think so.'

Cassie eased a smoking scone onto Ruth's outstretched

plate. She smiled around at the room, as if it was a person towards whom she felt oddly drawn.

'I like this place. It's got good vibes.'

'Vibes?'

'Emanations – vibrations – you know!' She sipped at her tea. 'My dad's pretty hung-up about most things – but I expect you already know that.' She looked suddenly angry. 'He objects to me living with Julian, when all summer long he's been here with you, going at it like knives every night.'

Ruth could feel the blood drain out of her face. 'Well, not every night,' she murmured.

'Sorry,' muttered Cassie. She scrambled across the carpet to Ruth, and flung her arms around her. 'Didn't mean to upset you. 'Specially now.'

Ruth studied the girl's upturned face. 'You're fond of him, aren't you?'

Cassie nodded. 'He's unhappy. He's always been unhappy. It makes him bloody-minded and defensive.' McInnes's daughter looked younger, and not at all sophisticated. 'You could help him if you really wanted to, Mrs Flemming. Why don't you?'

Ruth split a scone and then worried at the crumbs on her plate with a buttery knife. 'Perhaps he's a hopeless case,' she said lightly.

'Rumour says you're a damn nice woman; too good for the bastard McInnes. Are you? Is that the real problem? Are you too good for my old man?'

The question hung dangerously between them. Ruth felt an urgent need to justify herself. She said, regretfully, 'I'm afraid he's not quite the sort of man I've been accustomed to dealing with.' She felt the explanation to be inadequate, but Cassie seemed to understand; she nodded in perfect comprehension.

'I can just imagine,' she said, 'the impact a man like my father would have on a woman like you.' She impaled another scone on the prongs of the fork, and held it out towards the fire. 'Have you ever seen my home, Mrs Flemming?'

Ruth hesitated. 'I went there last summer – to fetch some clean clothes for your father.'

'Pretty deadly, isn't it?'

'I once lived in a house like that,' said Ruth, 'where the

146

furnishings had taken over and become more important than the people.'

'That's it, exactly!' Cassie patted the old leather chesterfield. 'It's different in here,' she said slowly, 'I can lie on the floor if I want to. Drop my crumbs on your carpet.'

'Is that why you live in a squat?'

Cassie buttered a scone, and considered the question. 'It's more complicated than that. Dad disapproved of Julian because he's a drop-out. So I dropped-out too. We stepped off the merry-go-round together.' She looked rueful. 'Trouble is, too much freedom can be pretty exhausting. When there's nobody around to tell you what you mustn't do, then oddly enough, you no longer want to do it.' She shrugged. 'We shall go back to University in the autumn. If they'll have us.'

'That will please your father.'

'You think so?' Cassie sounded uncertain. She glared at Ruth as if expecting condemnation. 'That house. I couldn't stay in it, you know. I found my mother's body in that bathroom.' She laughed, hysterically. 'It was insensitive of him, to say the least, don't you think, to expect me to, in the circumstances.'

'Your father feels as badly about it as you do.' Ruth began to defend McInnes with a passion that surprised her. 'He hardly ever went back there, any more. He blames himself much more than you could ever blame him.'

'But I don't blame him. I saw what my mother's sickness did to him. She couldn't help it, but that only made it worse. It would have been easier for us if we could have held her responsible for all our problems.'

Ruth rested a tentative hand on the girl's black hair. 'I've done my share of blaming,' she confessed, 'and not always very fairly. Your father pointed that out to me.'

'You actually find time to talk to one another, do you? It's not been all holding hands in the moonlight? Dad's never had that in his life before. A woman he can talk to.'

'We disagree about most things. As a matter of fact, I don't see him much, these days.'

'You've given him the elbow?'

Ruth was confused. 'Well no – not exactly.'

'You've left him dangling then? He won't like that. He's the old fashioned sort. He'll insist on marriage.' Cassie

147

picked at a loose tuft in the carpet. 'I don't understand you. What the hell are you playing at with my father?'

'I – I can't decide anything,' stammered Ruth. 'not at this stage.'

Annoyed by Cassie's look of disbelief, she burst out, 'I've already been lied to by my husband and my sister. You can't imagine what that feels like! Oh, I suspected. But I'm a woman who can live with suspicion. It's the confirmation of it that destroys me.'

'But you've got to believe in somebody; especially when you don't have much faith in yourself, and you haven't, have you Mrs Flemming?'

Ruth said, 'I've made some mistakes; about other people's lives as well as my own. This time, I have to be quite certain.'

'I'd like to come and see you, later on. When you've got the baby.' Cassie stood up with a great clanking of ankle-chains and medallions. Attempting nonchalance, and not quite succeeding she said, 'I never had a brother or a sister. Be quite a far-out experience for me, don't you think?'

*Part Five*

# LEO DAYS

# 1.

Spring came back to the city, but slowly this year. The daffodils in her garden showed an inch of green, made promises to her, but did not keep them. So she bought easy blooms from St Joseph's market. Ten yellow blossoms, tastefully arranged before a mirror, at once became twenty. To cheat, she discovered, need not be such a painful business after all. It just required forethought, and a certain knack. Perhaps everybody cheated, just a little, but called it by another name: rationalisation, compromise; making the most of what was available, or on offer.

McInnes was on offer. Oh, she had him. In the palm of her hand, on toast, by the forelock. Any way she wanted him. A middle-aged policeman, sick to his soul, lonely, and looking for the reprieve, the second chance, the new beginning. It would be so easy to take this man for comfort – if comfort was what she needed? Or had she played the role of befriender for so long, and to so many people that it had become a habit she could not break.

She had said to them, 'Please come in. Do sit down. Why don't you tell me all about it?' She had tuned-in to despair, frustration, grief. Viewed panic and rejection without ever growing that extra hide of indifference recommended to her by Sam Bright, who had observed her vulnerability, and feared for her.

'Keep some strength for yourself,' Sam had counselled.

In mid-May the daffodil bulbs which had sulked in the frozen earth all winter, flowered unexpectedly for her. Late, and almost out of season.

Walking had become difficult. A slow amble around the square, and back through the churchyard marked out her limit. It was pleasant to stroll in the early mornings, before the city yawned and the gritty streets filled up with people. The fact of the baby still surprised her. It was like snow in August; something rare and precious. To be held in the hands and wondered at.

But the child, unlike snow, would not melt at her touch. Plans would need to be made, and contingencies reckoned with. McInnes made plans. He arrived late one night, and unloaded a small folding pram from the boot of his car. 'It's not very grand,' he apologised, 'but you won't have much space in this cottage. The body lifts off from the chassis,' he explained, 'it makes into a carry-cot so they tell me.' He'd touched the blue corduroy of the hood, and said tentatively, 'Be handy for holidays won't it? Or trips out in the car?'

Ruth walked slowly on that fine May morning. She gazed briefly into Mandelbaums' window. Paused at the larger antique shop to admire a display of old prints, and then crossed over the road to push open the heavy iron gates which led into the churchyard.

She had taken a few steps along the gravel, when a soft shimmering motion lured her down the wide path that led to the church porch.

Somebody had folded Della Smith neatly in the middle; like a used cigarette packet. She fitted exactly into the wire-mesh container, her feet and head half-concealed by accumulated rubbish. It was only her long fair hair spilled between the meshes that had ruined the murderer's ironic attempt to keep the churchyard tidy.

This time she did not hesitate: Ruth telephoned the Bridewell. They came with their sirens wailing, spilling out of cars like the cops in a television drama. Policemen ranged over the churchyard, the square, her cottage. They walked in through her open front door; they asked questions she either would or could not answer.

From her window she could see them placing a green canvas screen around the rubbish container. A policewoman called Jane administered sweet scalding tea laced with brandy to her; and rubbed at Ruth's hands until the chilled skin reddened. The memory of Della's fair hair, spilled between the meshes, would, she thought, stay with her for as long as she lived.

The clichés that made life bearable for other women had seldom helped her. People who inflicted hurt on others, were probably, she thought, themselves afraid. Policemen hurried in and out of her cottage, intent upon proving something. Conversations hummed all around her. 'She was asking for it,' said one detective. 'Oh, she had it coming to her,' said his colleague.

A dark blue trailer was towed into St Joseph's churchyard and left there. The lettering on its side said 'MOBILE POLICE UNIT'. Uniformed policemen and plain-clothes detectives skimmed in and out of its narrow door like worker-bees homing-in on a hive.

She remembered Della, her fair hair hanging loose, laughing across the upturned teacups. Billy Evans, saying, 'She do really need me, you can see that, can't you?' We are all, thought Ruth, responsible for one another. She moved uneasily on the chesterfield, and the baby, annoyed, kicked against her ribcage. The policewoman said, 'You appear to have run out of tea-bags and milk, Mrs Flemming.'

McInnes came into her house, swaggering a little, assuming his prior right of access. Well, he would, wouldn't he? For a policeman like McInnes, Della's death could afford his finest hour. Something to get to grips with was what he wanted; the dark deed, once accomplished, would allow him to demonstrate his skills.

'I don't know,' Mary Ryan had wept, 'why people like you can't prevent things from happening.'

They left her alone with him. She watched their blue-serge shoulders glide away beyond the churchyard wall; cap-badges glinting in the sunshine. She imagined the Inspector, laying a significant finger along his nose, and winking. 'Let's leave her to "Geordie",' he would have said, 'I have reason to believe that he knows this lady rather intimately already.'

Anger, she discovered, set the baby kicking. 'I know nothing,' she told McInnes breathlessly; both hands on her restless stomach. 'It's bad enough that I had to find her. I won't let you persecute me. Your men are treating my house as if it were part of the Bridewell. They've used up all the milk and tea-bags.'

He looked ridiculous in the low red chair, grey worsted knees almost touching his chin. 'It can't be helped,' he said calmly, 'so let's just get on with it, shall we? At approximately what time would you estimate that you found the body?'

He had flipped to a clean page in his notebook. There he sat, pencil poised, eyebrows lifted. His detachment appalled her. He was robbing poor Della Smith of her violent passing.

'She's not "the body",' Ruth cried, 'she's Della. We know her, McInnes. She knows us!'

'Knew,' he corrected. 'So let's be a bit more dispassionate about it, shall we? We'll not get anywhere at all if you go all hysterical on me.'

'I don't want to get anywhere, I don't want to talk about it. Della couldn't use the phone box, McInnes. It was too complicated for her. Did you even know that much, Detective Sergeant?'

He sighed. 'You have to tell me, Ruth. Anything you know or suspect. This is a murder enquiry. She was a silly little bitch, but even she didn't deserve to die that way.'

'Go away McInnes,' she said wearily. 'I'm out of touch with Mainstay. If Della had any enemies then I don't know them.'

Perhaps it was the truth? How could Ruth be certain that the people who consulted her office had confided all their secrets to her.

He shook his iron-grey head, and looked grim. 'We're not going to catch this "chummy". I can feel it.' He looked keenly at her. 'Examine your conscience, Ruth. Decide where your duty lies.' He snapped shut his notebook and stood up. He eased his long, bony spine into an upright position, and walked to the door.

'I'll probably be back,' he threatened, 'later on this evening.'

She had wanted to be alone, but after the front door had closed behind him she began to cry. Quietly at first, and then passionately.

'Sorry,' she told the baby, 'to inflict this upon you. But you do see, don't you, that it will have to be gone through.'

She went into the kitchen, coddled an egg and made oversweet cocoa with condensed milk from a tin. She felt shivery, and covered her shoulders with the fluffy pink blanket she had bought for the baby. The policemen's boots had left dirt on the floor; dark thick segments of glistening mud, picked up in the dewy churchyard, crescent-shaped, and stamped out with a wavy imprint. She thought about cleaning it up, but feared to bend over. The baby had gone quiet now; hardly moved a finger. She remembered Paisley, dragging shabby sandals through the Canon's gravel. 'Be careful, when you tell her,' she had warned the policewoman. 'She's not like other children; she's a gypsy. Tell her it was an accident, she'll understand that. Say that her mother was playing a game and something went wrong.'

When Sam Bright called in that afternoon, he found her still slumped at the kitchen table; the pink blanket drooping from her shoulders. He fetched tea-bags and milk from the corner shop; lit the fire and persuaded her to sit beside it.

'How could they have left you like this?' he demanded.

'I told them to go. I refused to see their doctor.'

Sam made strong sweet tea, and piled a plate up with biscuits. He put logs on the fire. 'I've taken Paisley to her grandmother,' he said, 'they'll be allowed to keep her in future.'

'Was she very upset?'

'Hard to tell. She's a funny sort of kid. Doesn't say much. She asked about you; asked me to give this to you.'

She unwrapped the newspaper parcel. Lying on the newsprint, damp and very grubby around the edges, was the yellow towel. Ruth touched it gently, and began to cry again. This time, her scalding tears hardly troubled the baby. It kicked her once or twice with an irritable heel, and then lay quiet.

Blame. The apportioning of it. The careful measuring process she had always employed; the doling of it out into deliberate parcels, making quite sure that each one took his well-deserved share. Until now, blame had usually been reserved for other people.

She remembered Della as she had been on that first visit; seated on a beercrate in the empty room, her purple suede fashion boots stretched out towards the fire. Ruth had brought comfort of a sort to Nelson Street. A red carpet, two armchairs; Billy Evans. She had tried to patch and mend the lives of Della and her child; had bought clothes for Paisley; allowed Della to tell her fortune; looked the other way instead of reprimanding. McInnes had warned her.

'McInnes warned me,' she told Sam. He refilled her teacup, his brown face pleated with concern.

'And so did I, gal! I told you, not so damned much involvement.'

Ruth said, 'I went to see the Taylors. I thought I might persuade them to take her back. I tried to warn her about the dangers of fortune-telling –'

'She was bound to die,' Sam interrupted, 'accident, disease, murder – it was inevitable. She'd antagonised so many people. Her husband, the Taylor family, Jack Hardy, the men she robbed, her neighbours. What chance had you got against all that?'

Ruth looked down at her altered body. 'I was hardly a good example was I?'

Sam laughed. 'Don't get dramatic and see yourself as a fallen woman,' he said bluntly. 'Your little fling with McInnes endeared you to Della. She was very fond of you, Ruth. Remember that.'

Every male in St Joseph's, from the age of fourteen and upwards, was questioned about Della. To quote his own words, McInnes 'turned Billy Evans inside out, drained him dry, and then stamped upon him.' But without results. Jack Hardy was also 'pulled in, filleted and boned', and then released to reflect on the folly of uttering threats against a gypsy in a public bar.

The Taylors broke camp and departed. After all, said McInnes smugly, there was no valid reason to detain them: and hadn't they already left enough rubbish behind them, one way and another?

An open verdict was recorded upon Della Smith; and Ruth Flemming's baby was born on the last day of May.

156

Superstition pulled her towards her own belief. Mrs Kindness Taylor had prophesied a child. 'Don' you give up too easy' she had said. 'You'm a good woman. The Lord'll look after his own.'

Ruth did what she could to assist the Lord. She cursed and sweated her way through a protracted labour. 'If I'm not exactly a good woman,' she told the astonished midwife, 'then I'm not really a bad one. I deserve this baby. The gypsy said so.'

When it was over, and the baby lay, complete and perfect in her arms, she felt no more than relief at a job well done; a prediction fulfilled. A son for McInnes. A brother for Cassie. The fears and the doubts would come later. She had never envisaged a male child. With a girl it would all have been so much easier; closer; less terrifying.

She considered her relationships with her father; with Harry; with McInnes. She was not clever with men; not manipulative like her mother and Georgina. 'I don't know anything about boys,' she told the baby, 'you frighten me. I'll never be able to cope with you. You'll grow tall, and aggressive, like your father. You won't love me.'

McInnes showed an unexpected sense of delicacy by failing to visit her in hospital. He sent flowers, daily; and wrote letters. It was almost a courtship. He was still curious about every aspect of her past life. He seemed to regard her as some rarely encountered species which must be studied closely while the opportunity to do so still existed. The letters were curiously revealing. He catalogued his movements with the stiffness and precision of a police report. It was only when writing about his emotions, that the official jargon failed him.

Mary Ryan, lately returned from 'Derry, visited the hospital one evening bringing Ruth a gift of several beautifully crocheted baby garments.

'Ah,' she said, tearfully, ''Tis only a mother knows what it is to suffer. You've come to it a bit late in life, Mrs Flemming, dear. But no matter.

Mary twisted the wedding band on her finger. 'Nothin' ever turns out quite what you expect, now does it? Bet you never bargained to end up with that ould McInnes. But there it is. That's life for you.'

Matt, so she said, had advised her to leave their three boys in 'Derry, for a while. Matthew Ryan was also making predictions.

'He says there'll be fighting in the streets of St Joseph's before too much longer. The local polis' have already got it in for our Mark. The coppers are stopping the kids on the pavements nowadays Mrs Flemming. Searchin' and harassin' 'em for no good reason.' she shook her head 'My Matt's right. They'll be safer in 'Derry.'

Sam Bright came to see her. He was deeply troubled, almost despairing.

'Things are hotting-up in St Joseph's,' he told her, 'coming nicely to the boil. It only needs one tricky incident between white and black ——'

'I can't believe it's that bad.'

'You've been away from Mainstay for quite a long time.' He laid a hand on hers. 'Can I give you some advice Ruth? Don't go back to your cottage for a while yet. You're looking pretty washed-out; you need some sunshine, gal.'

'But where can I possibly go with a ten-day old baby?'

'To your mother, of course. You can fly to Rome; no problem. I'll pack a suitcase for you. Get your ticket. Drive you to Manchester Airport.'

'I don't know, Sam. You've never met my mother, have you? She's not exactly the kind of women one turns to in a crisis.'

'For the sunshine, then! You know how you love the heat of summer. Get yourself a tan, Ruth. Give yourself some elbow room to think things over.'

# 2.

Her mother had aged. Italian food had thickened her waistline; the speedwell eyes looked weary, their lids like crumpled tissue-paper; her neck crêpey. But the piled-up curls were still determinedly golden; the legs long and slim in gossamer nylons.

'Darling,' she cried, from beyond the airport barrier, 'how wonderful to see you!'

Ruth had warned her mother by telegram of her imminent arrival. Phone calls to Rome were expensive, and explanations, she had thought, were bound to be protracted. As they moved away from the barrier, Mrs Maynard touched the fringe of the lacy shawl. 'Better give it back to its parents, hadn't you darling?'

'No, mother. He belongs to me. I brought him with me.'

'I don't believe you!'

'You'd better believe me; I'm breast-feeding, and that's no mean feat at my age.' Ruth's tone was crisp and dismissive. Her mother, pitched between chagrin and elation, concentrated at first on the unimportant.

'I don't know how you could undertake such a journey with so young a baby!'

'No problem, mother. The stewardess arranged a private corner for me to feed him, and I use disposable nappies. I was once a nurse, remember. I do know about babies.'

'I can't take it in, Ruth. I thought you and Harry had parted.'

'And so we have.'

'Then who's –?'

'– baby is it? It's mine, mother. That's all you need to know.'

'Are you going to remarry?'

'I'm still married to Harry.'

'That's not what I meant.'

'I know what you meant.'

'How you've changed, Ruth. I hardly recognised you.'

Rome smelled of diesel-oil and lemons. It was noisy and

159

exciting but artificial; and she could see why her mother loved it. The apartment was small; it had a balcony that overlooked a courtyard, ornate doors and ceilings, and floors of black and white checked-marble.

Ruth bathed and fed her son, and put him to sleep on a folded blanket in a wicker laundry basket. Her mother hovered distractedly about the baby, her rings snagging in the shawl, her long pointed nails threatening his eyesight. 'How clever of you to have a boy!' she exulted, 'I'm sure he'll turn out to be every bit as handsome as Harry.'

Her mother, thought Ruth, was in many ways inept. She only believed what she wanted to; had probably always done so. The realisation detracted from her glamour, made her seem more accessible. They were sitting in long cane chairs on the balcony, the laundry basket set between them.

'You didn't like me much, did you mother, when I was little?'

'Of course I liked you. What a silly question! But you were your father's favourite child. You looked like him; had his brains and temperament. He understood you.'

'Did he?' Then why, thought Ruth, did I never know it? Why did I always feel so alone, so frightened?

'Of course,' her mother was saying, 'George was a man who couldn't express his feelings. But it was you he turned to in the end. You he relied upon.' Her mother's features crumpled. 'How he would have loved your son, Ruth.'

Ruth said, 'Georgina was pretty. I always understood why you preferred her.'

'This business with Harry,' Mrs Maynard said, 'it wasn't my fault.'

'But you knew all about it, didn't you, mother'?'

'Georgina always confided in me.'

'Why did you let them make a fool of me? You could have warned me.'

'You seemed so detached about Harry. I thought you would deal with it in your own way: and I was here in Rome, remember.'

'Yes, you were, weren't you.'

Mrs Maynard said, 'I'm glad you came here; glad you turned to me when you felt unhappy.'

'I'm not unhappy.'

'Then why did you come here?'

Ruth looked down at the laundry basket. 'Motherhood,' she said, 'it's not what I expected.'

'It rarely is, darling.'

'I'm forty-one. I won't get another chance. I have to get it right with this child.'

'But you were a nurse. You know all about babies. You said so.'

'Can't you understand mother? Because you never loved me, I don't think I know how to love my own baby.'

The coral lips fell open; the blue eyes filled with tears. 'Don't blame me, Ruthie. I know that you think I'm a frivolous woman, and I expect you're right. But I did the best I could. I wasn't serious and clever, like you and your father. To tell the truth, I was always the teeniest bit frightened of both of you. I needed Georgina.'

She studied her mother; the frailty of her; and felt ashamed.

'You've never recognised love, have you Ruthie; even when it's been offered to you. You don't really know how to accept it.'

The days passed quickly. They hired a pram and her mother pushed it. They strolled in the morning sunshine, bought the English papers, and read them over coffee.

The baby curled his fat pink fist around Ruth's finger, and would not let her go. He was stronger than she was, or ever could be. One morning in early July her mother said, 'There's some trouble in your part of the world, darling.' Ruth took the newspaper from her: the headline read 'Rioting in St Joseph's, 35 policemen injured.' She read on.

'The trouble began when a white youth allegedly attacked an elderly Asian shopkeeper. It is believed that the Asian youths then grouped together and went after the skinheads with knives and missiles. The skinheads had barricaded themselves inside the Bird in Hand public house. The Asians attacked the pub, throwing bricks and smashing windows. The police were called, but the trouble had already escalated. Additional gangs of youths, both white and coloured, were coming in from other areas.' Quickly, Ruth scanned the columns of newsprint. 'Petrol bombs thrown at police. Pavements ripped up. An old people's home evacuated. Fire.

Looting. CS gas. Plastic bullets. Allegations of police brutality.' She looked at the date on the newspaper. July 5th, 1981.

The news from St Joseph's was already four days old.

Mrs Maynard drove her daughter to the airport. 'You will let me visit, won't you darling? I can't bear to be apart for too long from my grandson.' She gazed at the sleeping infant, who rode in a canvas sling suspended from his mother's shoulders. 'I still can't quite believe it, you know.'

'I'm still adjusting to it, myself.'

Her mother's enamelled prettiness was blurred for a moment by the unusual intensity of her emotion. 'Don't worry so much about loving this baby, Ruth. It's perfectly obvious that you're besotted about him. Just be willing to believe that he loves you; when the time comes.'

On the flight from Rome to Manchester Airport, her anxiety deepened. She worried about Sam Bright. McInnes was able to take care of himself; he at least was not partisan. He loathed all protagonists with an equal passion. She feared for the safety of the friends she had found in St Joseph's: Mary Ryan, Billy Evans, Jack Hardy. She prayed that her cottage had not been damaged; that the navy blue corduroy pram could still be positioned, as planned, underneath the pear tree.

The taxi driver, who had driven her from Manchester, looked around St Joseph's Square, and then at Number Seven Friar's Walk. 'Christ!' he muttered. 'Reckon you bin' lucky, missus. Somebody's bin' in an' boarded-up your windows; an' swep' the broken glass up.'

It was probably Detective Sergeant McInnes, she thought; still trying to protect his investment; still hoping to move in on her life; to take her over.

The cottage smelled of smoke, but, except for the smashed front windows, her home 'was intact. She placed the sleeping baby in the navy blue pram, and pushed him swiftly out of the square. She would need to fetch bread and milk before the shops closed.

The Bird in Hand pub had lost its roof. The gutted barroom where Cassie McInnes had once sung her ballad of sunshine, now stood open to the sky. Half demolished houses yawned in Trafalgar and Waterloo Street. On the white façade of the Mainstay building, yard-high slogans, in sweet-pea colours, had blossomed from aerosol cans; an odour of fear and burning hung about St Joseph's.

The corner shop was dim behind boarded-up windows. Ruth picked up bread and milk, and placed them on the counter. The Patels looked frightened, and distant; face to face with them, inside their looted shop, she hardly knew what to say. To enquire about their health was no longer reasonable, instead, she asked, 'Is the English language tutor I arranged for you, still calling?'

Prem Patel nodded. 'She come every Wednesday. Is very nice lady. I hope –' he waved a hand at the destruction '– I hope she come again to us, that she not be frightened.' Ruth reassured him, hoping that what she said was indeed the truth. Contacts between black and white she thought, would now be more important than ever. Links with the immigrant population, built up so carefully over many years, must be maintained at all costs. There was so much that still needed to be done here. Surprised; she could feel her old enthusiasm beginning to stir; her old interest in the work of Mainstay, returning.

The year fell away from its meridian, and the churchyard grass paled to faded ochre. The Leo days returned; her special time of full-blown summer, that spanned late July and early August.

Roses hung, limp and scented on her garden wall. The daffodil stalks still lay, brown end papery, in the borders. She positioned the pram in the shade of the pear tree; pegged nappies and little crocheted jackets on the clothes-line; and purchased a cat-net to protect her baby.

When McInnes came hammering on her door, she let him in without a word.

'You're back then?'
'Yes,' she said quietly, 'I'm back.'
'Where the bloody hell have you been?' he demanded. 'I made enquiries all round the district.' He sounded bitter. 'Your good friends wouldn't give me the time of day.'
'I went to Italy for a few weeks to see my mother.'

'Italy?' He seemed shocked. 'I came to the hospital, to fetch you, but they said that you had already left.'

'I wanted to be on my own,' said Ruth, 'I had things to think over.'

'So had I,' roared McInnes, 'and I didn't need to sneak off to Italy to do it.' The skin around his lips and nose had whitened, and she moved rapidly to place the width of the table between them.

'Oh, you eluded me very nicely,' he went on, 'quite the professional, aren't you, when it comes to avoiding a confrontation?'

'I made my plans well in advance,' she murmured.

'And they didn't include me? My God, Ruth – you must really hate me.' McInnes pulled out a chair and sat down quite suddenly. He placed both elbows on the table and rested his head in his hands. Once again his face had that raw, stripped look about it.

Ruth filled the kettle and remembered last summer. Nothing much, she thought, had really changed between them.

'You look well,' he said grudgingly. 'Motherhood seems to suit you.'

'Did you think that it wouldn't?'

'You've still got that secretive look; as if you know something that I don't.'

She smiled. 'How observant you've become in the past twelve months.'

He said, with difficulty, 'I'll resign the Force, if you want me to.' He paused, clearly expecting some comment from her. But she remained silent. 'You remember that fire in Waterloo Street? We got nowhere with it. A few agitators were rounded-up and kicked out of the district; but that was last year's spot of bother. The real action started up while you were away. We've had three weeks of race-riots.'

'Yes,' she said, 'I've seen the destruction; and my mother takes the English papers. I read about it.'

'It was bad, Ruth, and it's not all over yet. We ought to consider moving out of St Joseph's. It's not a safe place to live in, any more.'

'But it never was,' she said calmly.

'Look,' he insisted, 'I've been thinking about it. We could

move to the country. Buy a house in a village. Somewhere safe for our – for the child to grow up in.'

'No,' said Ruth, 'that's no answer. This is our slot, we belong here. Can't you see? Running away will solve nothing. We should still be the same two people. There's work to be done. We are needed, McInnes.'

'So what in hell do you want?' he burst out. 'I've been beating my brains out just lately, wondering how I can please you.'

'There's no need,' she assured him. 'I've never been so happy.'

'Oh,' he said heavily, 'well that's canny – for you. You've got your cottage, your baby, your grandmother's bit of money. But where do I stand, then? What about me, Ruth?'

'What about you, McInnes?' Her voice sharpened. 'Stop whining damn you. You're beginning to sound just like Harry. You once told me not to buy love, and I really listened to you, Michael. I took note. I learned. Love has to be earned hasn't it? But you and I haven't even begun to work on it yet.'

He lay on a clean white sheet, eyes tightly closed, small chest heaving gently beneath a blue nylon romper. His rounded limbs were gold from the sun, and his soft dark hair stood out in little damp peaks all around his head.

They gazed down upon him. For a moment, all their anger was suspended. Ruth looked up at McInnes. He had grown new bitter lines around eyes and mouth in the past few months. There were several tiny creases at the points of his shirt collar. She would, she thought vaguely, really have to start doing his ironing for him. The policeman was trembling slightly. He latched his gaze to a patch of worn grass at the end of her garden. 'What?' he asked tentatively, 'have you decided to call him?'

'Michael,' she said. 'I thought that perhaps, we ought to call him Michael.'

**THE SUMMERHOUSE**
**Val Mulkerns**

'A remarkable book, full of insight and feeling . . .'
EVENING PRESS

It crouched forlornly in the kitchen — a crumbling fretwork
summerhouse, a symbol of failure and decay, perfectly
appropriate to the family that drifted round its
disintegrating form, sniping bitchily at each other.

Eleanor, beautiful, frustrated, feeding on her contempt for
her spineless husband Con; Margaret, mother of Martin,
slowly sinking back into the clinging folds of her family
from which she had all too briefly escaped; their mother,
senile and overbearing; Hanny, spinster daughter, finding
her only satisfaction in eroding her sisters' confidence
and self-image; and Ruth, Martin's wife, a crisp if timid
observer of the lethal family minuet . . .

Told in the voices of five separate but intertwined
characters, THE SUMMERHOUSE evokes the lives of an
Irish family whose tragedies and occasional joys will haunt
every reader.

'evocative'
THE IRISH PRESS

FUTURA PUBLICATIONS
FICTION
0 7088 2623 7

**HAPPY FAMILIES**
**Nigel Gray**

'a powerful indictment of our society'
YORKSHIRE POST

Paul has survived the bleakest and saddest of childhoods.
His unloved mother left him unloved, and a string of
children's homes left their mark. But he is an optimist and
with the birth of his illegitimate child he determines to
build her a good future.

But as life slowly starts to crumble around him the
memories of his childhood overwhelm him. He feels
increasingly trapped by the society he's a part of and by
his frustrated efforts to break free from the cycle he was
born into . . .

'an authentic and rare writer'
JOHN BERGER

'writes with the compassion of a saint and the practicality
of a plumber'
EDWARD BOND

'impressive'
SUNDAY TELEGRAPH

'a brutal novel, also a work of tenderness'
NEW STATESMAN

'raw energy'
STANDARD

'worthy of respect'
IRISH PRESS

'A laureate of desolation'
OBSERVER

'Mr Gray has a rare talent'
SUNDAY TRIBUNE, DUBLIN

FUTURA PUBLICATIONS
FICTION
0  7088  2995  3

## LARKSLEVE
**Patricia Wendorf**

Eliza Greypaull knew she was no beauty, but she was determined to make a success of the arranged marriage to her weak-willed, dissolute cousin Philip, for the future of Larksleve depended on it. The lush Somerset farm would divert Philip from the fleshpots of Taunton and would be a home for the next generation of Greypaulls.

Yet despite her gown of golden silk, and the dowry of sovereigns sewn into a velvet bag, she couldn't suppress a stab of envy at the glowing happiness of her friend Meridiana. Using gypsy spells and incantations, the impetuous Romany had ensnared the man of her choice, but she was to pay dearly for her love . . .

The coral pendant encircled these two families. Its powerful magic caused pain and joy in equal proportions, and its purpose would only be worked out over several generations.

'Most compelling reading . . . the characters are beautifully realized and contrasted'
ROSEMARY SUTCLIFF

'Truly magical, the work of a very special kind of writer. I can't remember when I last read a story that so captivated me . . . I felt privileged to read it'
SARAH HARRISON

'Written with a native's instinctive feel for the language, traditions and landscape of the West Country'
MAIL ON SUNDAY

FUTURA PUBLICATIONS
FICTION
0 7088 2860 4

**BLANCHE**
**Patricia Wendorf**

'Patricia Wendorf is a marvellous story-teller . . . the novel
is absorbing'
PUNCH

Blanche Greypaull is a wild, independent beauty, her hopes
high as she sets out for London. Leaving behind her the
years of poverty in the dark hovel of Taunton's slums and
her unhappy childhood on Larksleve — the family home
which her drunken father squandered — she seeks her
fortune, determined to find a wealthy husband. For hasn't
she promised to see her mother in silk before the year's
out? And doesn't she herself yearn for diamond rings, rich
gowns — and a man who will lie down and *beg* for her?

But as she heads for the grandeur and splendour of the
city, Blanche is soon to learn that passion can burn just as
strong in her heart as ambition . . .

'a very memorable heroine'
ANNABEL

FUTURA PUBLICATIONS
FICTION
0 7088 2861 2

All Futura Books are available at your bookshop or
newsagent, or can be ordered from the following address:
Futura Books, Cash Sales Department,
P.O. Box 11, Falmouth, Cornwall, TR10 9EN.

Please send cheque or postal order (no currency), and
allow 60p for postage and packing for the first book plus
25p for the second book and 15p for each additional book
ordered up to a maximum charge of £1.90 in U.K.

B.F.P.O. customers please allow 60p for the first book,
25p for the second book plus 15p per copy for the next
7 books, thereafter 9p per book.

Overseas customers, including Eire, please allow £1.25
for postage and packing for the first book, 75p for the second
book and 28p for each subsequent title ordered.